"What

Anne asked Sam, her voice low and soft.

He took a deep breath and let it out slowly. She could see him silently counting to ten and was glad she was driving him as crazy as he made her. "That's a foolish question to ask me," he said.

She stepped toward him, surprised at her own boldness, but realizing it was necessary for her to make the next move. "Tell me what you want."

He took hold of her by the shoulders to hold her away from him, but his fingers caressed her skin. "I want you. Every night I've dreamed of you in your lace-and-satin gown, in this room. I've imagined *everything* I could do to you."

"Yes?" Her voice was breathless. "What would you do?"

"Make love to you. Slow and soft. Fast and hard. There isn't an inch of you that I wouldn't kiss."

"Yes… What else?"

He scowled at her but she saw desire in his eyes. She smiled and he scowled more fiercely. "I'd make you scream when—"

The smile dropped off her face but she moved even closer to him. She licked her dry lips. "Promises, promises. Prove it."

tear that pink dress off her and devour her. None of the

Molly Liholm admits that all she really knows how to do with computers is type, but the idea of a baby with a web page seemed like a fun twist to the baby-abandoned-on-the-doorstep idea. After all, computer genius Sam Evans only understands logic and machines, until he's thrust into the messy life of baby Juliet and nanny Anne Logan. "The BACHELORS & BABIES miniseries," Molly says, "is such a natural combination of sexy men and adorable babies. What's more fun than having a big strong hunk of a man reduced to a quivering pile of Jell-O by a baby's giggle?"

A native of Toronto, Canada, Molly works in the publishing industry when she's not playing on her computer.

Books by Molly Liholm

HARLEQUIN TEMPTATION
552—TEMPTING JAKE
643—BOARDROOM BABY
672—THE GETAWAY GROOM
706—THE ADVENTUROUS BRIDE

BABY.com
Molly Liholm

HARLEQUIN®

TORONTO • NEW YORK • LONDON
AMSTERDAM • PARIS • SYDNEY • HAMBURG
STOCKHOLM • ATHENS • TOKYO • MILAN • MADRID
PRAGUE • WARSAW • BUDAPEST • AUCKLAND

For Birgit Davis-Todd.

Thanks for being willing to read my first book
so many years ago and for all the good advice!
It's been a pleasure working together.

ISBN 0-373-25845-3

BABY.COM

Copyright © 1999 by Malle Vallik.

All rights reserved. Except for use in any review, the reproduction or
utilization of this work in whole or in part in any form by any electronic,
mechanical or other means, now known or hereafter invented, including
xerography, photocopying and recording, or in any information storage
or retrieval system, is forbidden without the written permission of the
publisher, Harlequin Enterprises Limited, 225 Duncan Mill Road,
Don Mills, Ontario, Canada M3B 3K9.

All characters in this book have no existence outside the imagination of
the author and have no relation whatsoever to anyone bearing the same
name or names. They are not even distantly inspired by any individual
known or unknown to the author, and all incidents are pure invention.

This edition published by arrangement with Harlequin Books S.A.

BABY.com is a registered trademark and registered domain name of
eToys Inc.

® and TM are trademarks of the publisher. Trademarks indicated with
® are registered in the United States Patent and Trademark Office, the
Canadian Trade Marks Office and in other countries.

Visit us at www.romance.net

Printed in U.S.A.

1

THE BABY CRIED.

Sam Evans frowned at his computer screen. If he changed the cosine to $y+2$, his calculation should work. He quickly typed the changes into his program and then waited for the computer to make the calculation.... Damn, the wrong answer flashed on the screen. He'd been stumped on this problem for a week, but he knew he was getting closer. If he changed the variable of y to x, then he could... The baby cried again. Sam looked up, scowling at the interruption. He needed quiet, no distractions, no people, so he could concentrate on his work.

"Ellen, will you go see what that infernal racket is?" he shouted before he remembered he'd said goodbye to her—he checked his watch—over three hours ago. He always lost track of time once inside a programming equation.

Three hours was nothing. On more than one occasion he'd worked over forty-eight hours straight—if he was left alone. That's how he liked it.

The only person who ever dared to pull him away from his beloved numbers was his cousin Ellen. Sometimes, when she left to close one of their business deals, she placed alarm clocks in different locations in their office, set to ring at varying times, all part of her plan to jar him out of his concentration. Otherwise, she would claim with her bright smile, she might return four days later to find he hadn't moved from his chair. Someone had to take care of him, Ellen said. As his partner, she figured it was part of her job description.

Sam listened for the cry. He was sure the noise he'd heard wasn't an alarm clock. Then he smiled, pleased to have come up with the solution. "Damn the girl, she's bought one of those novelty clocks," he muttered happily to himself and turned his attention back to the computer screen. Except he couldn't concentrate. He heard the plaintive wail again and couldn't get the image of a lost baby out of his mind.

Don't be ridiculous, he told himself. There weren't any lost babies in Portland, Maine, especially not in the neighborhood that housed his office and his home. Still, he closed the computer file, turned off the machine and looked out of the window but, other than the dark waters of Casco Bay, he didn't see anything. Or was that a person moving behind a bush in the park across the road? He focused…no, it was only a bird taking flight.

"This is why I don't spend my days dreaming out of windows," he muttered. "It's foolishness." Plus he liked his world of numbers and logic much better.

What had Ellen said to him as she'd left? She was going to call him once she arrived at her hotel in Seattle. Considering it was a four-hour flight from Portland, Maine, to Seattle, then adding the time she needed to get to her hotel, she'd be calling him around midnight—not long enough for her to have to set the alarms. Five hours was really a warm-up stretch for him, so Ellen wouldn't have been worried.

She looked after him, and he appreciated it. What they said about blood being thicker than water was only too true. If anyone had told him twenty years ago, when he and Ellen used to spend summers in Portland with their aunt Gwen, that they would be partners in a very successful business enterprise, he would have believed them. Ellen and he had shared a bond from that first summer they'd spent together. Both of them lonely and miserable, a pair of misfits who had fit together. They had shared all their dreams and, after every miserable winter apart, they had begun to build upon their dreams to create a business together.

All of Sam's good childhood memories involved numbers. He had loved their beauty and logic. There were no lies with numbers. To hide from his parents' endless fighting, he learned to stay in the library until closing time and then to hide in his room, so that his parents might forget about him. His teachers recognized his genius for mathematics and accelerated him, but that meant he became the child prodigy in a class filled with students much older than he. Once again, he was an outcast.

Ellen had pushed him to ignore the taunts of his much older classmates and to excel. That first summer together had happened because he'd failed a class—he'd been so bored by it, he'd spent that period hanging out at the local video arcade instead—and his parents had despaired of what to do with him, a big, awkward, socially inept and hostile boy. Aunt Gwen had invited him to come visit her and his cousin. His parents had been relieved to get rid of him so they could fight to their hearts' content. Sweet Ellen, with her glasses, lank hair and baggy clothing hadn't despaired of either of them. If anything, she had driven them both. Sam to his Ph.D. in artificial intelligence and she to her business degree from Harvard.

Then they had struck out on their own, to make it big. And they'd succeeded beyond their wildest imaginings. The past seven years had been the best years of his life.

So why had Ellen looked at him rather wistfully after she'd closed her briefcase and asked if he was happy?

He'd been lounging on the couch in their large work area, watching Ellen arrange all of her presentation materials for her Seattle trip, part of his concentration, as always, dealing with the problems of his next project. Ellen's question had taken him by surprise and focused his attention on her. He took his feet off the coffee table and straightened. "Of course I'm happy. We're doing what we always wanted to do. You run the business end of our company and I get to think and invent."

"And that's enough to make you happy?" Her brown eyes were worried and she fluffed her bangs with her fingers.

Ellen played with her hair whenever she was troubled. "Is something wrong, Ellen? Are you worried about the deal with ComputExtra?"

"No." Ellen waved off that topic, her mother's emerald ring catching the sunlight pouring in through the large windows of the Victorian building. Ellen fiddled with the lock on her attaché case and then sighed. "It's just that sometimes I wonder if we aren't fooling ourselves. We've accomplished what we fantasized about as children."

Sam nodded. "We formed our partnership."

"Right, we're rich," she muttered and then turned on him, her face alive with some emotion. "But is this enough? All we do is work. You create and invent, I market and negotiate the deals."

"They're more than just deals," he'd insisted. "A lot of our programs have helped medical researchers—"

"And help children learn, and your probability programs on sudden weather shifts will help future generations plan for severe weather occurrences like El Niño. I know all that and I know we're doing good. Moreover, we give away almost as much money as we make." She let out a sigh. "It's just that I'm thirty-two and I go to bed alone every night. Not to mention there was Martin's wedding last week."

"Don't tell me you're pining for him." He hadn't thought she'd been in love with Martin. "You dumped him over three years ago."

"I didn't dump him. We both agreed that we were better off as friends. I'm not in love with Martin."

"Well then, what is it? If you think we're making a mistake in selling our program to ComputExtra—"

"No, nothing's wrong." Ellen pulled on her gloves and straightened her scarf against her brown cashmere jacket. "I'm just being silly." She walked over to the window looking out at the bay. "Sometimes I forget how beautiful our view is."

Now Sam was concerned about her. It wasn't like Ellen to stare out the window to see the view. Usually she saw the future. But he decided to try to humor her. "We chose to set up our operation in Portland because it's a beautiful place to live."

"I know. We could be anywhere but we picked Portland because it's so picturesque and friendly. All of my good childhood memories are of us in this place. Aunt Gwen and Theodore may have moved to Chicago, but I always think of this place as home." She turned away from the window and picked up her briefcase. "Now we're doing exactly what we dreamed of as kids but we never take the time to enjoy it."

Sam got up from the sofa and stepped toward her. Something was very wrong. "Ellen, what is it?" Once she told him, he was sure they could fix it. There wasn't anything he wouldn't do for Ellen Evans.

She shrugged her shoulders. "Nothing. I'm just in a funny mood. I'll call you as soon as I've settled into my hotel." She patted him on the cheek. "Don't forget to eat." Ellen had left and he'd gone back to his desk and worked until the sound of a baby crying had disturbed him.

"You're being ridiculous," he told the empty room. "There's no baby—" Another wail filled the air. "What the hell?" He got up and looked outside the window. He saw the bay, a few boats on the water, but no people on the street. "Because it's dinnertime. Families are home together having dinner, getting ready to watch 'Wheel of Fortune.'" But still Sam felt uneasy and he left the office area of the large house. He decided to go to his own apartment, nuke a frozen dinner and turn on the sports channel. Out of habit, he locked the door to the offices of E², the name he and Ellen had christened their software company. They had chosen it years ago when they realized that developing computer programs was what Sam would do while Ellen ran the business end of things. The name, E², played on their initials as well as Einstein's famous formula of $E=mc^2$, achieving a strong identification for themselves in a very competitive market. As usual, the marketing strategy had been Ellen's.

Sam considered E² his baby—and the only baby he wanted.

He stopped in the hallway of their shared Victorian when he reached the front door. He had the apartment on the second floor while Ellen had taken the smaller third floor and attic, saying she liked its coziness and the view. What the hell, he might as well open the front door and prove to himself that he was hallucinating. Ellen's peculiar behavior must have rubbed off on him.

He opened the door and looked out at the empty street. There were a couple of cars parked across the road, where the parkland ran along the bay. "Nothing," he muttered. "I am an idiot—" The very definite cry of a baby stopped him and made him look down. On the porch, inside a white wicker basket, lay a pink blanket and shiny little face.

"What the hell?" Sam felt dizzy as he kneeled down to touch the basket. He wasn't hallucinating. It was real. A white wicker basket with a yellow bow. A soft-looking wool blanket inside. And a baby.

Stepping over the basket very carefully, Sam moved onto the porch and looked around. Still no one in sight. He leaned over the railing and poked the bushes. Nothing.

"Come out, I can see you," he shouted, his voice sounding rather desperate to his own ears.

No response.

"Martin, this is a stupid joke. Stop trying to change my life." He was greeted with silence and remembered that Martin and Cynthia were on their honeymoon in Aruba.

This couldn't be happening to him.

Something moved in the bushes to the right of the porch and he raced down the stairs, jumping over the last two steps to land dead center in the bushes. He heard a squeak and felt the brush of something by his leg as a squirrel ran for its life. "Damn." Sam refused to believe that all he had heard was a squirrel. Squirrels didn't drop off babies on doorsteps, the stork did that, and even he—a man who didn't pay much attention to the everyday world—knew the story about the stork was make-believe.

He searched every foot of his property, turning around in circles until he became dizzy. Nothing. He found no one hiding behind a tree, laughing at the practical joke being played on Samuel F. Evans.

No one was around except the baby in the basket on his front porch.

Slowly, carefully, he went back up the steps. Despite blinking several times, the basket and baby were still there. He wished he could go inside and pretend he'd never heard the baby's cries. Then someone else could come by and find the baby and be responsible for it. He knew absolutely nothing about babies. Moreover, he wanted to keep it that way.

Awkwardly he picked up the basket and went back inside his house. Somehow, the house felt different. He took the steps to his own apartment, careful not to trip over anything and drop the baby, unlocked the door to his apartment and entered his home. Everything looked the same, but it wasn't. He shook off the weird feeling and went down the long corridor to the back of the house, put the basket down on his kitchen table and then stepped back. Now what was he supposed to do?

"A note. There's always a note with a baby in a basket," he said, remembering the plot of several movies he'd seen on late-night television that involved abandoned children, and moved closer to the table, peering inside the wicker basket. All he could see was a pink ball of fluff. Awkwardly he poked his finger under a corner of the pink blanket and searched, but he found nothing except the baby's foot. The baby kicked him.

"Damn. I'm sorry," he said to the baby, "I didn't mean to swear, but I'm not used to little people like you." He was barely used to people. In fact, now that Sam thought about it, he'd never been alone in a room with a baby before. He leaned his large body over the infant who scrunched up its face and made a gurgling sound.

"What? Are you all right?" The baby repeated its actions and then waited for Sam to respond. "You should have a note," he told the child, wishing the little thing could talk. At what age did they begin to speak? he wondered, realizing he knew absolutely nothing about babies. Who would have left a baby on his doorstep? What if he hadn't been home? While it was early fall, the nights became cool quickly. This little bundle of pink fluff could have become seriously ill or worse.

Sam shivered and blocked out the image his imagination had conjured up. Instead, keeping his voice jolly, he continued looking through the basket. "There is a fine tradition of leaving a note, maybe even a locket, with a baby on a doorstep. Perhaps they didn't tell you the rules."

He found an odd package at the baby's feet and he pulled it out, glad that he was right about part of this mystery. But when he opened the brown paper bag he found six disposable diapers. He stared at a diaper and its plastic tabs, wondering exactly how it all worked. Hopefully, as soon as he dialed 911 and contacted the authorities, he wouldn't have to learn. Changing diapers was not in his life plan. Along with the diapers were two baby bottles filled with what he assumed was milk. Everything was so tiny in his massive hands.

The baby smiled. The little rosebud mouth fluttered and Sam felt a curious sensation in his stomach. The big brown eyes looked up at him and then blinked, exhibiting long, dark lashes. Sam felt another peculiar sensation, this one further up in his chest around his heart. The baby waved a chubby fist at him and, without thinking, Sam extended one of his big fingers so that the little thing could touch him. As the small delicate fingers grabbed one of his, Sam felt a band tighten around his heart. "Oh, no, you don't," he said as he finally saw the note that he'd been looking for. "There it is," he exclaimed too loudly, and the baby scrunched its face in complaint, the lips trembling, the rosebud mouth opening.

"Hush, little baby, it's okay. I was just being too loud," he cooed, cursing himself. He had to remember that he must seem like a giant to the little thing. He towered over most adults. "Everything will be okay. No one's going to hurt you." The baby smiled at him again, sighed and then closed those big brown eyes. He waited for the baby to fall asleep and, after a few minutes when he thought the baby might be sleeping, he unpinned the note from the blanket.

The baby didn't stir, so he unfolded the note and read the message, hoping for enlightenment. A small part of him had been wishing that the note would be addressed to Ellen. He knew the baby wasn't hers. Even as caught up in his own world as he got sometimes, he would have noticed something that obvious. Besides, when it came to Ellen, he was pretty in tune. For example, over the past few weeks, he'd begun to realize that she wasn't happy, but he also didn't know what the source of her troubles was.

So, no matter how absentminded and removed he was

from the day-to-day world that most people lived in, he would have noticed if Ellen were pregnant.

Still he'd been hoping that some friend of Ellen's had left the baby on their doorstep. It was *their* doorstep, after all. To his dismay, the typed note was addressed to him. Moreover it was short: *For Sam Evans. From www.baby.com.*

"What the—" He stopped himself from swearing in front of the baby again. He needed to get to his computer and access the baby's homepage. *The baby's homepage?* The situation was becoming more and more surreal.

Who would deliver him a baby with an internet address? He no longer doubted that the child was meant for him, the computer connection proved it.

After all, he was one of the leaders of the information age. In college, he had been wooed by every large computer company, and afterward had been approached by every firm in Silicon Valley. But he'd always preferred being independent. Ellen called him a loner.

He liked being responsible for himself and only himself. And Ellen, of course, but she was strong and knew how to stand up to him and to deal with him when necessary. They had the best kind of partnership—a meeting of minds along with the tie of family. She was the only person he wanted to be connected to. He'd learned better.

Only now someone had given him the responsibility of an infant.

He headed back toward the office, to his most powerful computer, and had reached the door when he remembered the baby on his kitchen table. He couldn't leave the child alone. What if the basket fell off the table? Without stopping to think too much, he scooped up the basket, holding it straight out in his arms, trying to keep it steady as he walked so as to not wake up the baby.

Back in the office downstairs, he booted up his computer with one hand while putting the basket at his feet on the floor. He looked down at the pink-cheeked little infant who had woken up and was returning his stare with equal curiosity. "Who are you?" he asked. The baby didn't answer so he turned his attention back to the computer, which knew how to communicate with him. He understood rational, logical thought. People were too often beyond his comprehension.

In minutes, he had accessed the baby's homepage. The baby screamed. He looked down at the infant from whose rosebud lips eminated a cry that would have made a primal scream therapist proud. He held his fingers to his lips, "Hush, this is what I do. I'm just going to click some keys and find out—" The baby wailed louder.

"What's wrong?" he crouched forward, putting his face close to the infant's. The baby opened its mouth further and screamed at a pitch and volume Sam found astonishing for anything so small. Fervently wishing for a mute button, he made a hushing motion with his hands. "Shh, you need to be quiet so I can learn who you belong to." The child ignored him and scrunched its face, turning a peculiar shade of purple. This couldn't be good for the little thing.

As the baby continued to cry and grow a darker shade of violet, Sam stared at it helplessly. "What do you want?" he demanded, raking a hand through his hair.

The baby wailed in response and punched its tiny fists at him.

Unable to take it any longer, Sam got out of the chair and began to pace as the sobs and hiccups continued. He wished he'd been around a baby at some point in his life, but he'd always managed to avoid any such entanglements. When he'd been engaged to Darlene, he'd looked inside a baby stroller or two, trying to imagine what it would be like to be a father, but had never felt any paternal stirrings. Obviously, the biological clock stirrings were female only. He'd assumed that Darlene would take care of that and eventually he would get used to the baby. Now

he was having to get used to a baby a lot sooner than he'd
expected.

As the baby continued its display of obvious displeasure, Sam sighed and then went back to the basket. People were always holding babies; indeed he remembered Walter, one of their workers, spending hours holding his little baby—a boy, he thought—singing and playing with the child. How hard could it be?

Taking a deep breath, Sam scooped the child out of the basket. The head, he remembered. He had to support the head. With some maneuvering, he managed it so that the baby's head was cradled on his elbow and the rest of its body was hugged against his chest. The baby made a cooing sound, looked up at him with those big brown eyes and sighed. Now what? he wondered once he finally broke the spell the baby had cast on him. He managed to sit down on his chair, at his desk, staring at his beloved computer. He had only one hand with which to keyboard. The baby gurgled. He looked back down at those dark eyes but broke contact before he could be distracted again. He needed answers, not this strange warm feeling he got whenever he looked at the baby.

With his one free hand using the computer mouse, he clicked the Enter command and the screen lit up with a number of questions.

"A security check. Clever." He answered the questions: the color of the baby's blanket—pink, the color of the bow on the basket—yellow, hair—blond curls. Then he was past the security check and gained access to the web page. He blinked and read the page again feeling light-headed.

"Welcome, Sam Evans," he read. "Thank you for agreeing to be my father."

"Don't be ridiculous. I haven't agreed to anything. I have no intention of being a father. I don't want to be a father." He found he was shouting at the computer and stopped. The baby looked at him curiously but didn't complain. "Sorry," he said anyway. "Whoever set this up is crazy. Maybe I should stop reading right now and call the police." The baby looked back at him intently, trusting him to do the right thing.

No, he couldn't just abandon the child to the proper authorities. Someone had entrusted the child to him so that the child-care workers wouldn't be responsible for the baby. He glared back at the computer screen. "I want to know the child's name."

He scrolled further down the screen and found the stats on the baby. "So you're a girl," he told her, glad to have some kind of association with her. According to her birth date, she was five months old. Five months today. "Happy birthday," he said, searching for her name, but it wasn't listed anywhere. He found instructions on diaper changing, food preparation, bathing instruction and other references on where to find information on babies, but no mention of her name.

"I can't just call you baby girl," he told her. He'd named each and every one of his computers; the little femme fatale needed a name. He looked at her and considered as she studied him with equal concentration. She reminded him of someone.

Sam froze as a new thought hit him. Surely he couldn't really be the father of this adorable little girl. Who was he dating—five plus nine—fourteen months ago? Around that time, when he'd been developing the program that Ellen was presently selling to ComputExtra, there had been Louise, or was it Lulu? But they'd only gone out twice and then he'd gotten obsessed about his new program that would make time management easy for even the most computer illiterate and then he'd...? He'd forgotten to phone her. He hadn't seen her after their two dates and he'd certainly forgotten to have sex with her.

After that was a brief interlude with Marianne six months ago, but that had ended after a month, and while

---

they'd had some very good sex, she couldn't have had his child and delivered it to his doorstep in only five months. Plus, he always took precautions.

The baby scrunched her eyes at him and he remembered his first-grade teacher, Miss Juliet Sommers. She had had the same brown eyes and rosebud lips, and he'd fallen as desperately in love with her as any Grade One boy could. Especially a very lonely and out-of-place Grade One boy. Juliet Sommers had been nice to him, he remembered. "Juliet," he told the child. "I'm going to call you Juliet. Until I find your real parents and learn your real name."

Which brought him back to the search for her parents and the rest of the web page. A little voice inside him said it was time for him to call the authorities; they would know what to do. Did he dial 911 or the regular police? "The regular number, I guess, since it's not an emergency," he told Juliet who smiled trustingly back at him.

The authorities would come and...? Social workers and foster homes. He'd watched television cop shows—he knew the drill. And what if they never found little Juliet's parents? He'd heard too many horror stories about the system. Sam knew how awful it could be with your natural family; without one, it would be even worse.

He had an alternative, he realized.

Someone had entrusted the child to him. Could he really turn his back on her so easily? In front of him on the computer screen was all the information he needed to take care of Juliet for one night. He could feed her and change her diapers. All kinds of ordinary people did it every day.

At the bottom of Juliet's web page there was the promise to send him a new e-mail in the morning about the child. He was an adult male of thirty-three with a doctorate in artificial intelligence. He was considered a visionary when it came to imagining what computers could do for people. Surely he could look after one little baby girl for one night.

Sam touched Juliet's nose with the pad of his index finger. Her skin was as soft as rose petals. She giggled. He'd keep her, just for tonight. First thing in the morning, he'd read the new electronic post and find someone to look after Juliet. One night, no more. "Well, Juliet, it looks like it's just us two. I don't know what's going on here, but I'm not going to abandon you. I know what it's like to have bad parents, so trust me, I'm going to check yours out completely before I give you back."

Juliet nodded, as if she had found her very own Romeo, he thought. Which just proved how ridiculous he was becoming. And then he remembered that love story had a very sad ending.

"Not for you," he promised her, realizing he meant every word. "You're going to have a happy ending."

2

THE BABY CRIED.

Sam rolled over in bed, pulling a pillow over his head to try to block out the horrendous noise. He'd had the weirdest dream. He'd been a kid and someone had forgotten a doll at his house. He'd trekked up and down streets knocking on doors, trying to return the toy. The doll was very valuable and it was up to him to get it home, but no one wanted the doll...

He rolled over again and cursed. The damn dream had made for an uneasy sleep; he felt as if he'd woken up several times during the night. Sam sat bolt upright, realizing his dream from last night wasn't only a nightmare but also hard, cold reality.

Juliet was crying.

"Coming, coming," he shouted kicking off the sheets, grabbing a robe to wrap around himself.

Juliet cried louder and Sam practically ran to the other bedroom where he'd put her in a makeshift crib—a drawer from a dresser. Again, he'd relied on his memory of TV and movies. Parents always put the child in a separate room—a nursery. Of course, if he kept the child for another day, he would put the baby's basket in his room. It would save the three trips he'd made rushing out to respond to Juliet, once to change her, twice to feed her. During the first feeding, he promised himself that as soon as any bureaucracy opened its doors at nine in the morning, he'd be there to thrust Juliet into their waiting arms. Then he'd burped her as his instructions had told him to and she'd fallen asleep in his arms. He'd ended up holding her for he didn't know how long, enjoying the smell and feel of her. Having that tiny, precious bundle trust herself completely in his arms had been moving. The feelings she created in him began to explain why women wanted children. Why there were so many articles on the infamous ticking biological clock.

Parenthood, however, wasn't for him. Today he was going to figure out what to do with Juliet. Diva, the computer program that Ellen was selling to ComputExtra, needed fine-tuning and he wouldn't be able to work on her if he had to look after an infant.

"Come on, Juliet." He chucked her into his arms, holding her head in his left palm and talking softly into her ear. "Let's find you something to eat." Juliet agreed and, after feeling that her bottom was wet, he changed her diaper— it was only a matter of simple engineering and manual dexterity, as well as a fair degree of baby powder, it turned out. "Now, time for food." Juliet made a funny sound and Sam looked at her. "Oh, no, you don't. You had me up half the night explaining computer formulas and theorems to you. Plus calculus. I've never met a woman with such an appetite for calculus. How about if we just talk this morning?"

Juliet looked at him, her cupid-bow lips curving in agreement. Sam was relieved. Last night he'd run through every mathematical theory he remembered when Juliet had woken up cranky. He'd tried telling her a story but couldn't remember any, and his deep singing voice only scared her. In desperation, he had began to talk through his latest programming problem and Juliet had settled down immediately with a look of interest on her face.

He rubbed his nose along Juliet's as they walked down the long narrow hallway of the Victorian to his kitchen in the back of the house. Ellen always complained that he'd done nothing with his part of the house, but he didn't really see the need. The basic architecture of the building, including its cornices, leaded glass and fireplaces was well-crafted. He loved the design and, other than that, didn't care. His kitchen held a stove, fridge and dishwasher, plates and pots. He didn't see any need for knickknacks or matching dish towels or whatever it was that women spent hours obsessing over. His mother's home had matched, had been redecorated every two years according to the latest decorating magazines, and he'd never felt at home in it. No, he liked his bachelor mismatched splendor. Anytime a woman he dated began to move his furniture and buy place mats, he knew their relationship was coming to an end. Of course, if he were honest, in the past few years, he'd barely let any woman into the bedroom.

Except for Juliet, of course.

"Welcome to my kitchen." He took the last of the baby bottles from the fridge—he'd have to drive to a supermarket for formula—and put it into the microwave. Then he began to make coffee, pouring water into the machine and then carefully measuring out spoonfuls of the elixir of life.

"First we're going to have our breakfast and then I'm going to phone Ellen and ask her if she knows anything about you. Yes, I realize it will be only five in the morning in Seattle, but if I'm not getting enough sleep, I don't see why she should be. Don't give me that look—all cute and innocent. You're the one who interrupted my sleep." He chucked her under the chin and her lips fluttered as a smile flew across it. He tried to imitate her and she waved her fists at him. "Pretty easy to entertain, aren't you?"

Sam realized this was the longest conversation he'd had with a woman across a breakfast table since…well, probably ever. Usually he forgot about the woman who had shared his bed, thinking about the day's work ahead instead. At first Darlene had complained, but eventually she'd shrugged and claimed she would get used to it.

She hadn't. All of his attributes that she had assured him

would make up for his lapses hadn't balanced out in the end.

The doorbell rang and Juliet cried. "What the—?" He stopped himself from using his regular vocabulary in deference to the little girl nuzzling against his shoulder. Who could possibly be at his door this early? He checked the clock and it read eight-thirty. His friends and colleagues were used to his late working hours and never dared to wake him at this ungodly hour of the morning. "Fudge," he told Juliet, believing he may have heard Mary Poppins say some such thing in a movie he once saw as a child. Mary Poppins? He needed his coffee and his regular life back.

Sam waited for one of his employees to answer the door—Walter and Susan were always the first to arrive. But when the chime rang again, he remembered it was Saturday. Ellen had decided to fly out to Seattle on a Friday so she had the weekend to acclimatize to her surroundings and to size up their potential partners. No one was downstairs to answer his doorbell.

Maybe Juliet's parents had regretted their decision and had arrived to take her back into their loving hands. Still holding Juliet against his shoulder, Sam hurried down the stairs toward the door. He wouldn't hand her over without any questions, but he did want to hear their story and rid himself of this overwhelming responsibility. If he wanted children, he'd have his own. "Get ready to say bye-bye," he told Juliet and with the words "Hello, Mommy," he flung open the door.

A woman with curly, long blond hair smiled back at him. She had nice, even white teeth. "Hello, Daddy," she answered, her blue eyes sparkling. Juliet waved at the woman. Good, the baby wanted her mother. He held out the child and, with a look of surprise, she took it. "I'm Anne Logan." She cradled the baby naturally. She wasn't beautiful, but there was something very maternal and appealing about her.

She seemed about five-seven, a good half foot shorter than himself, but holding the baby in her arms she looked like she could take on the world—and win. There was no wedding ring on her finger, he noticed. Maybe her boyfriend had run off with the baby, abandoned it on Sam's doorstep and the determined and resourceful Anne Logan had traced the baby here. She looked like a woman who would be determined and resourceful. Even now, reunited with her daughter, she was very calm.

Sam found her very appealing—because she had arrived to take back the baby.

"Won't you come in?" He stepped away from the door into his nice, safe home, even nicer now that the baby mystery was about to be solved. "I just made some coffee."

"That would be lovely." Anne Logan gazed curiously at him with her bright eyes, but didn't say anything as she followed him up the steps to his second-floor apartment into his kitchen and took a cup of coffee. "Just milk, please," she requested and then looked around the room. "You're not married," she finally said.

"Is it that obvious from my kitchen?"

"Yes." Anne sipped her coffee and waited for him to say more, but he had no more to say. Anne Logan didn't seem like the kind of woman to abandon her baby on his doorstep, yet she might have done exactly that. Juliet wrapped one chubby fist into Anne's pink cardigan and pulled on a button. "Hush, baby, it's all right. Aren't you the cutest little thing?" Anne smiled at the baby and then looked up at him. His breath caught in his throat for a second at the unconditional love on her face. Insanely he wondered if she looked at the baby's father with the same kind of love and felt a stab of jealousy.

"What's your daughter's name?" Anne asked.

Sam spluttered out the coffee he'd just sipped. "What?"

Anne arched a brow. "I wanted to know her name."

"She's your daughter!"

"Good heavens, no. I would never be that presumptuous. As her nanny, I'll be very close to her, but I would never attempt to take the place of her mother." Anne Logan tilted her head as she gazed at Sam sympathetically. "I'm sorry, has her mother passed away?"

"No. I don't know." Sam stood and began to pace. His kitchen still looked like his kitchen, but now it included a lovely blonde dressed in pink who claimed she was the nanny. This crazy situation was getting even crazier. He closed his eyes, but when he opened them, there were still the three of them trapped in his own private domestic hell.

Anne cooed to the baby and held her protectively as she eyed him warily. "Perhaps I misunderstood something about the situation? I'm usually quite good with details, but lately, I've been a little distracted what with visiting my brother, trying to get all my stuff into storage and then advertising for a new job. My last job was in Seattle and when it ended I realized I finally had time to visit my brother. And then this job came up. That's why this opportunity seemed so, so opportune. A golden opportunity just falling into my lap." She smiled at him. "Sorry, some people, my brother, Davis, actually, tell me I ramble."

"Are you sure you're not Juliet's mother?" Sam's hope faded away. Competent Anne Logan looked like she'd be such a good mother. Like she would have some really good logical reason for leaving her baby with him. Like she would have ensured he would know what to do with the baby via instructions on the internet. She looked like a woman who knew how to sew baby clothes and surf the web.

"Juliet. That's a lovely name."

"It was also the name of my first-grade teacher," he told her distractedly.

"Sweet. You had a crush on her."

"So did every other little boy in her class."

"Mr. Richardson was my Grade Four crush. You know if you moved the plant next to that shelf, the indirect light would be better for it. Do you mind?" she asked as she tucked the baby next to her with one hand and then moved the plant to its new home. "You'll find it grows a lot faster and will turn a deeper green."

Sam was surprised to see he had a plant. Ellen must have put it there and, since it was still alive, she must have been watering it. He wanted to understand what was going on. "If you're not Juliet's mother, then who are you?"

"I'm the nanny. Why do you keep asking me if I'm her mother?" Anne kissed the baby's fist and turned her enquiring, intelligent eyes on him.

Sam was completely bewildered. He also wondered why a small part of him was happy that Anne wasn't the mother. This was the wrong time to be attracted to a woman. Moreover, Anne Logan was the wrong woman to be attracted to. He'd made his mistake with her kind once, and he learned from his mistakes. "The nanny? I don't need a nanny."

"You have a baby," Anne pointed out. "That is usually the first requirement for a nanny. Although I did interview with a man once who wanted..." She blushed. "Never mind. If you have a daughter and are a businessman, then you'll probably need a nanny."

"Juliet isn't my baby. I found her last night. I was hoping you were the mother who had come back for her child."

"Someone left Juliet with you?"

"Left her on my doorstep."

Anne Logan blinked in surprise. "But that can't be. I was hired to be her nanny."

Finally a clue. "That's right. Who hired you?"

Anne shook her head as if she couldn't believe the situation. "Gwendolyn Parker. She interviewed me last week and asked me to arrive early today. She said that you were a busy businessman and wouldn't be good at hiring a professional to look after a baby. I thought that you were divorced or widowed. Who is Mrs. Parker?"

"She's my aunt. Which reminds me…I need to use my computer." Sam bolted out of the kitchen, racing down the stairs two at a time, back to his office. He had his computer booted up within seconds and accessed baby Juliet's homepage.

Good morning Sam! The words on the computer screen were cheery. He could hear his aunt's voice.

I trust the nanny, Anne Logan, arrived bright and early this morning. Click here for her résumé and references.

He ignored that suggestion and scrolled down further to find out what Gwen was up to.

The baby is my present to you. You've been isolating yourself from the world too long. The only person you seem to truly care about is your cousin, Ellen. Well, being the meddling aunt that I am, I've decided those walls need to be knocked down, with a bulldozer, if necessary. The baby is the bulldozer. Anne Logan is to help along the way—I'm not foolish enough to abandon you completely—plus I don't want you handing the baby over to the authorities. I have my reasons, and I'll get to them shortly.

You'll find Anne a godsend. She came very highly recommended.

Back to the baby. I know her mother, a teenage runaway. You know that sometimes I volunteer at a youth shelter; I met Veronica there. She was seventeen, scared and pregnant. She left the home before she delivered the baby. We were all worried, but it happens. You start to get used to it. Or you deaden yourself so you can keep going on. When Veronica—she likes to be called Ronnie—disappeared, I was sad but not surprised. I was surprised, however, when she arrived at my apartment six months later, with her unnamed baby. I let her stay the night and we talked about her giving the baby up for adoption. That's why she hadn't picked a name—she didn't want to get too attached.

Sam felt a trickle of sweat roll down his back as he realized he'd picked a name for the baby. No, that was nothing to worry about. His aunt wasn't going to make him change his life. He liked his life the way it was. He'd made the kind of life he wanted—having a baby around for a day or two wasn't going to change him. He continued reading.

The next morning Ronnie was gone.

I could have gone to the authorities, but you know what a soft heart I have and how I like to meddle. If I hadn't I never would have gotten to know you or Ellen so well, and I like to believe that I did help the two of you. Both of you were so lost when you first started spending the summers with me. If I wasn't such a busybody I probably would have given up on the pair of you, but I was so convinced I could do something good for you that I continued.

I believe the same thing about Ronnie's baby.

Ronnie is just a scared little girl herself and she doesn't know what to do about her child. The idea of having to make a choice is overwhelming her. But I know a very nice couple who would make very good parents. Now all I need is for Ronnie to sign the adoption papers, which means I have to find her.

Thank goodness, Gwen knew people who wanted to adopt Juliet. The tension in his shoulders eased slightly. Juliet would go to a good home—after he checked out these people himself.

If the baby goes into the system I'll have no control over who adopts her and I want that control.

Plus, I think the baby will be good for you. She'll make you think about something other than your computer programs. There is a reason it's called artificial intelligence, after all. As your aunt, I can say such things. That was me hiding in the bushes last night. My but you gave me a fright when you almost caught me. I needed to make sure you found the baby.

Anne Logan is here to help you. I was lucky to hire her under such short notice. When her brother told me that she'd recently become available, I took it as a sign that my plan would work out.

I'll contact you again tomorrow.

Sam stared at the computer message in bemusement. This couldn't really be happening to him. Aunt Gwen had to have completely lost her mind. He loved her, but could he really go along with what she wanted?

Still he did owe her. If she hadn't interfered in his life and in Ellen's he didn't know how he would have turned out. His IQ was at the genius level, but he'd been an emotional wreck until Aunt Gwen had taken over. Sam looked back at the computer screen and sighed. He owed Aunt Gwen big time and no matter how crazy he thought her scheme was, he'd try to hold up his end.

At least she had sent him Anne Logan. With her looking after the baby, his life would hardly be interrupted.

He looked up to where Anne was standing by one of the shelves studying his books. Dressed in a pink, belted dress that flared from her hips, a matching cardigan and her blond hair cascading down her back, she looked very soft and feminine. The dress ended at her knees, revealing very nicely shaped calves. He felt a sudden urge to run his hand along her legs and stroke the inside of her knees. Ridiculous. He wasn't lusting after Anne Logan—she wasn't his type at all.

Sam liked tall, sophisticated brunettes. All of the women he dated were successful businesswomen. They understood about deadlines and were willing to schedule dates in between them. If they planned to have children, they also planned to hire a nanny. None of his dates had any desire to be supernanny. Sam appreciated women who used their minds, who were determined to blaze their own path of glory.

A woman who liked taking care of other people's children? He didn't understand that lack of ambition at all. He smiled trying to picture career-driven Ellen being friends with Anne Logan. Impossible.

Darlene was the one woman who reminded him of Anne Logan and she was also the biggest mistake of his life. Luckily he had found out the truth about her before it ended up costing him too much.

Anne turned around and found him staring at her. Instead of being nonplussed, she smiled and he felt his pulse pick up. "Did you find out the information you needed on your computer screen?"

"Yes, my aunt Gwen, the woman who hired you, thinks I should look after the baby while she finds Juliet's mother."

Anne blinked at his surprising words, but she schooled her face to reveal none of what she was thinking. "Are you going to?"

He could tell she wanted to say a lot more, but was forcing herself to remain silent. "Yes. She's my aunt and I care a great deal for her." He realized he would do anything for his aunt; after all, she had saved his life. He shrugged. "Plus, as crazy as her plan sounds, I trust her judgment."

She nodded, and pointed to the bookshelves. "You're a computer programmer of some sort?" Anne asked. "Your books and state-of-the-art equipment make me think you know how to do more than just surf the net."

"Yes, my cousin Ellen and I own a software company."

"That's nice that you like to keep business in the family. My brother does something with computer things as well, but whenever he tries to explain what he's working on, he usually loses me after the first minute. In fact, he was the one who recommended I take this job since I was looking for something short-term. He lives in Portland. I was visiting when I got your aunt's call. He would love your office. Can I see what your aunt wrote?"

He replayed her torrent of words trying to find the logic of her thought pattern. "Of course." Before Sam could move out of the way Anne leaned over his shoulder to read Juliet's web page. He smelled vanilla, lavender and warm female skin, and found himself lost looking at her elegant neck. Her skin was ivory, as soft-looking as a rose petal. He wanted to run his fingers along her neck to see if it could possibly feel as velvety as it looked. He kept his hands to himself.

Her gaze raced over the screen and she smiled. "Your aunt is a very caring woman. I thought so when I interviewed with her. Otherwise, I wouldn't have agreed to come out here to discuss looking after your baby. Why don't you go ahead and take a look at my résumé?"

"What?" Sam asked, feeling confused once again.

Anne reached into the large blue bag that he didn't think went with her pink dress at all and yet did, at the same time. "Here's my résumé and my references. Please feel free to call as many of my former clients as you like. I don't usually agree to an assignment that will last only a few weeks, but your aunt was very convincing."

Sam looked at the résumé in puzzlement. Ellen always hired their employees. "I thought Aunt Gwen had already hired you."

"No." Anne shook her head emphatically and her lovely blond hair flew around her face. He would love to see it flying around her face as he made love to her. *Stop that.* Lusting after a nanny was a very bad idea. Nannies were traditional women: the home and hearth type. He was not the home and hearth type. He watched her lips as she answered, "I agreed to come for an interview. It's important to see if our personalities mesh if I'm going to look after your child."

"Juliet isn't my child."

"She is for now."

Ignoring Anne's words, and the chill that raced down his spine, Sam perused her résumé. Anne Logan was almost thirty years old and had been working as a profes-

sional nanny for over eight years after graduating from
Browns College with a degree in child care.

"Why children?" he asked.

"I love babies and children. Everything about families,
in fact."

"Then why don't you have your own? Isn't looking after other people's families second-rate? You are thirty, after all."

"I'm twenty-nine. My birthday isn't for another
month." She took a deep breath and Sam refused to notice
how the bodice of her dress moved. "Being a trained child-
care professional is a very honorable profession. As a
child, I had a wonderful nanny and she helped me become
the woman I am today."

"A woman who looks after other people's children." He
couldn't help needling her and her eyes flashed with anger.

"I plan to have my own children someday, but I intend
to marry the right man, first."

Sam was furious with her; she was one of those women
who had dreamed of getting married since she was a little
girl. Just like Darlene. "So you're looking after other people's children and on the hunt for Mr. Right. Do you have
a list of requirements for the future Mr. Logan?" he asked
her harshly, his tone laced with cynicism.

Anne opened her mouth and then closed it so quickly
that Sam knew he'd hit a nerve; she did have a checklist of
requirements for the potential husband. He wondered
how high up money was on the scorecard.

"Let me guess," he continued. "You're looking for a
mate who, one—" he checked the points off on his fingers
"—has similar interests to yours. Two, wants children.
Three, has a good sense of humor. Women always claim to
want a good sense of humor, although if he's rich enough
that requirement disappears very quickly. Four, you want

a man who will make family his number one priority, and last, someone who's financially secure."

Anne glared at him. "You are an infuriating man, Mr. Evans. I think you should check my references and leave my personal life out of this." She crossed her arms and then continued between gritted teeth. "From what I've gathered from your aunt's note, at least I have a personal life. I'm not afraid to admit I'd like someone to share it with."

Anne positively glowed with anger. If she hadn't been holding Juliet in her arms, he thought she might have grabbed the thickest computer book she could find and brained him with it. Stop trying to anger her, he told himself. Just because she was the kind of woman he avoided like the plague, didn't mean he shouldn't hire her.

Her résumé was impressive and included the Swedish ambassador to America. "Do you speak Swedish?"

"I picked up a fair bit of the language during my stay at the embassy, but the ambassador liked me to speak English with her children so that they could learn American colloquial expressions."

Sam knew all about parents who constantly wanted to better their children rather than let them actually enjoy their childhood. "Your last job with the Stones was only four months long. Isn't that a very short period of time?"

Anne kissed Juliet on the top of her head. "She's so beautiful." Then she looked him straight in the eye. "I don't like to accept any assignment that's less than two years, because it's important to have the time to make a difference in a child's life. My nanny lived with us until I went to high school."

"I had a succession of them." He pressed his lips tight together so that no more of his private thoughts could escape. The next thing he'd be saying was that he'd like to tear that pink dress off her and devour her. None of the women he dated ever wore pink. "Why was that job so short?"

"The couple was having marital problems and have separated. Mrs. Stone decided to find alternate child-care arrangements." She looked at him, understanding crossing her face. "You don't approve of nannies. Not just me, but all of us. You had some kind of bad childhood— probably you were a child genius and your parents ignored you, farming you out to the hired help. Oh, I'm so sorry. Davis is right, I do ramble."

He hated the look of sympathy that crossed her face. "Perhaps I don't really believe in paying a stranger to look after your baby."

"But you need me."

"Juliet isn't my daughter."

"She could be. She has the same brown eyes as you."

Sam looked at the baby with surprise and Juliet looked back at him as if she, too, wanted to check out the comparison. "See," Anne said. "She has the same way of opening them wider when she's concentrating."

"I didn't think babies spent a lot of time concentrating. I thought they just existed, breathed and slept and ate and pooped."

"Aha, you had to change several diapers last night." Anne smiled at him and he had to press his lips together in his best scowl in order not to smile back. "For a baby everything is new. Can you imagine what it must be like to have to figure out everything? It must be a little like when you create a computer program that does something new."

"At least I have the beginning steps. I know the math and the language." He wasn't about to give in so easily, although he thought Anne's comparison was a good one. Unable to resist, he touched Juliet's chubby, little fist that she was waving about.

He wanted Anne to stay. She would take care of the

baby and he could work. He would barely know they were in his house; it was a big house, he could keep his distance from them. "You win. Will you agree to stay and take care of Juliet?"

"You've been very rude to me. I have half a mind to say no."

"Please," he asked.

She looked at him with what appeared to be surprise on her face. "Juliet is adorable and your aunt did say you were going to be difficult." She shook her head as if she thought she were making a mistake, but then she smiled at him. "I'd be happy to take the job—temporarily."

3

JULIET CRIED. LOUDLY.

Anne picked her up, holding the baby against her chest. "It's okay, Juliet, dinner's almost ready. You don't need to cry." The little girl continued to scream. To distract her, Anne faced her toward the large kitchen table and patted the child's back. "There now doesn't the table look nice?" she crooned. Juliet looked up at her, stopped her screaming and gurgled in agreement. Smiling, Anne tickled Juliet. Juliet waved a chubby fist at her and she pretended to eat it, smelling the sweetness of the baby. Oh, how she adored babies—their smells and sounds and need for you. All the babies she had looked after were special, but there was something about Juliet she couldn't define. Every time Juliet smiled with those rosebud lips and twinkled her brown eyes—which unnervingly reminded her of Sam Evans—she felt the baby take hold of her heart. "I'm only going to take care of you for a little while, love. Don't go making me fall in love with you." Juliet looked at her and then shook her head ever so slightly. "Well, you're not playing fair. At least I won't be falling in love with your sexy but grumbly guardian." She knew better than to make a mistake like that. Paul Stone had taught her the foolishness of mixing personal feelings with business. Luckily he had only wounded her, and a lot of what he had wounded had been pride. Her heart had only taken a minor beating.

Now Sam Evans would be different. My but he was tasty…only she wasn't biting.

"Tasty," Sam said behind her and she jumped. "Sorry," he said. "I didn't mean to frighten you. I was checking out Juliet's web page again—Aunt Gwen hasn't made any further progress in finding the mother—when the aroma of home cooked food pulled me out of my office. I don't think I've ever smelled anything so good in my apartment. Whenever I cook something, all I smell is burnt food." He walked over to the stove, opened the oven door and peered inside. "A casserole," he said with awe.

Surely the man has tasted casserole before? It was the staple of every homemaker's menu plans. Except he seemed to have had a less-than-wholesome upbringing, so maybe home cooked meals weren't familiar to him.

Calm down, she told herself. She wasn't going to start feeling sorry for Sam Evans. Her brother had told her how successful his company was—and warned her that Sam had a reputation for never dating any one woman for long. Even Davis worried about her romantic life. Well, there was no need for any of them to worry.

All she needed to do was stop behaving so ridiculously. Sam Evans was not the most perfect specimen of maleness she had ever slapped her eyes upon. So then why had she been so delighted to find absolutely nothing feminine in his apartment? Certainly no woman lived here now and hadn't ever, it appeared. "Have you always lived alone?" Now what was wrong with her? She didn't usually say what was running around her head. If she did, no one would ever be safe.

Because she was a meddler. Even worse, a manipulator. And nobody was safe once she'd decided she knew what was best.

Oh, she didn't tell her victims that she knew what best for their lives, but she was worse than a matchmaking grandmother and global bank CEO combined. That was why she had decided to become a nanny, so she could organize whole families. And she loved every second of it.

And now she was wondering about Sam Evans.

This house told her a lot about him. She knew that he and his cousin owned the building with their business on the first floor. Sam lived on the second floor with a large living room at the front of the house and a kitchen at the back. On the east side Sam had a large spacious room for himself. She had only snuck a quick look, but the solid colors and plaid bedspread in his room had screamed masculinity. No woman slept there regularly.

The other two rooms on the west side were basically leftovers. Anne would have turned one into a dining room; she could hold the most wonderful dinner parties in a house like this. While one room was functionally furbished as the spare bedroom, the other was a big junk room. She liked the view from the junk room and had decided she'd take that one for herself. The nursery would continue next door, where Sam had originally put Juliet to sleep in a drawer. The man was certainly resourceful. He might say he knew nothing about babies, but he was adapting very well.

But Davis had told her the man was a genius, so she shouldn't be so surprised. He hadn't told her that Sam Evans was so big, so male, so sexy. Anne didn't like to fall for stereotypes, but most of the computer gurus she'd met—and she'd met many because of Davis—had been more geeky than Greek godlike. She looked at Sam standing next to the stove, an expression of wonder on his face. He was huge, at least six-three she figured, because she stood five-seven without heels and he positively loomed over her. Big shoulders and a chest just made for a woman to sleep on.

Pulling her thoughts away from their dangerous direction, she opened her mouth and said the first thing that popped into her head—not for the first time, unfortunately. "I'm going to sleep in the bedroom next to the nursery."

"What?" Sam looked at her with suspicion.

"I'll have my brother drop off some clothes and stuff for me tonight and then I'll get the rest of my things tomorrow. Davis will be pleased to meet you. He showed me an article about you in some computer magazine, I can never keep the names straight, and said I'd be reading about him someday, too."

He frowned. "You're going to sleep here?"

"Of course. I am a *live-in* nanny." He was beginning to annoy her, which was a good thing. This man really seemed to have considered very little as to how Juliet would affect his life. Which meant he never really thought about children or families, which meant she wasn't going to fall for him. He most certainly had none of her requirements for a good husband. "Would you rather I left every day at five and let you take care of Juliet until the next morning? I could post messages on Juliet's homepage instructing you on how to take care of her."

"God, no." He practically shouted. Juliet made a noise and turned her head, looking toward Sam. "No, I need all the help I can get. As you may have noticed, I don't know much about babies."

At the look of panic on his face, she bit down on her lip to hide her smile. "Few men do before they become fathers, but then they pick it up very quickly."

"Well, I only intend to keep Juliet for as long as necessary. Aunt Gwen can move quickly when she wants to. I'm sure she'll track down Juliet's mother in a day or two and then we can return to our regular lives."

Anne wondered just how speedily Gwen Parker would find Juliet's mother—and what exactly her plan was. As a meddler herself, she recognized a fellow meddler's handiwork. Clearly, for some reason, Gwen thought that her nephew needed a baby in his life. Based on the impression given by his apartment, Anne thought he could use any kind of personal touch.

No, she wasn't going to be around long enough to try to fix Sam Evans's life—no matter how much she suspected he needed it. Or how sexy his mouth was.

"I hope you're right about Gwen being able to find Juliet's mother quickly. The longer we have her, the harder it will be to say goodbye. Here—" she held the baby out to him "—can you hold Juliet for a few minutes while I finish dinner?"

Juliet fit into the crook of his elbow perfectly and, for a moment, his harsh features softened. Anne felt a pull on her heart and turned away. She was only in this man's house for a day or two to help out during an emergency. And she'd be able to spend some time thinking about what she wanted to do next with her own life. As much as she loved her work, lately she'd begun to feel something was missing, which was probably why she'd let herself fall for Paul Stone.

"Dinner smells wonderful. I usually just microwave something," Sam said.

"I saw your large supply of frozen foods. You're living up to the cliché of the single man almost too well. It's a good thing I'm used to this from Davis. If I taught him to cook, I can show you a thing or two."

"Is it part of your duties to cook dinner?"

"No, but we have to eat and you seemed lost in your work."

"It was only the smell of casserole—" again, he said the word almost reverently "—that pulled me out of my work." He shrugged regretfully. "I can lose myself for hours and not notice anything when I'm trying to work out a problem."

"Davis can be like that, too. I'll cook dinner some nights, but you'll get your full turn. I don't like those frozen things."

Sam looked down at Juliet and then back to her. Anne was trapped by his gaze and felt... Whatever she had almost felt was gone. Careful, she told herself. Sam Evans, a big wounded bear of a man, could draw her to him, but she didn't want to have her heart broken again.

Something about him called out to her. It was the way he'd watch Juliet and looked so surprised at what she did. Juliet clearly loved being in his arms and, while he was a natural with her, he was so tentative—not something she expected from a man of his size. She wouldn't mind changing places with Juliet, though. Stop that, she told herself. She should keep her mind on dinner and off Sam's impressive body.

While she found him physically desirable, there was a guarded hurt that called out to her soft heart. People in Sam's past he'd trusted and loved had wounded him.

Juliet cooed, calling Sam's attention back to her, and Anne was glad for the excuse to hurry to the oven and pull out the casserole, hoping her flush would be mistaken for the heat from the oven.

"I have a feeling my life is about to change more than I would like," Sam said to her back.

She faced him, holding the casserole as a shield between them. "I think that may be what your aunt Gwen had in mind."

"I'm afraid you might be right. The table looks very nice."

It did, too, Anne thought. Sam had some very nice navy place mats and she had found some white napkins and then two blue Depression glass wineglasses as well that she'd filled with water. Inside a large blue mug she'd added some white flowers she'd picked from the front yard. She rather thought that Ellen was the only one who did any gardening. Sam was not the cultivating type.

"Sit down," she said. "If you'll keep Juliet for a while longer, I'll serve dinner. You had a lot of fresh vegetables in your fridge, so a chicken and vegetable dish was easy." Sam did as she requested, talking to Juliet in a surprisingly musical voice for such a big man, as if he'd been taking care of babies his whole life.

But Sam Evans wasn't interested in babies, she reminded herself. And she wanted a man who wanted a house filled with children.

Once she'd served them dinner, she took Juliet away from Sam and placed her in the basket the little girl had arrived in, then put the basket on the floor close to her chair. "The basket and the impromptu bed you made out of a drawer will work for tonight, but tomorrow we should go shopping for a few baby things. I looked through the Yellow Pages and there's a good secondhand baby store listed, so we'll be able to keep the cost down."

"The money doesn't matter." He looked up from the food he'd been devouring and scowled at her.

"But you're not going to have Juliet for all that long," she pointed out. "You'll need a car seat and a stroller and a crib—and that's if we only have her for a week or two."

"A week or two?" He paled. "I thought Gwen would be able to find her mother in a few days."

"I hope so, but I think you have to be prepared for the real possibility that it might take much longer." She stood up and walked to the counter where she had written down their shopping list and her schedule. "Here's some of the items you need and my suggested schedule for dividing up Juliet's time."

He took the schedule, read it quickly and then fixed his fierce gaze on her. "I thought you were hired to look after Juliet."

"I was, but it's not a twenty-four hour a day job. I like to take a half day on Wednesdays and then two evenings a week, preferably Thursday and Friday."

He continued to stare at the list as if that held the answer to something that was on his mind. She hoped it was her. She didn't like to think that the curious tingles she got around him were only one-sided. "Why those nights?" he demanded.

"They're good date nights. My brother has several friends he's offered to fix me up with, so I'm looking forward to my time in Portland. Don't look at me like that. You're the one who thought I had a checklist of husband requirements. Well, I do. And in order to meet Mr. Right I have to be out there. Dating." She glared at him daring him to be sarcastic. "If I were like you, working all the time, I'd never meet anyone. It's not like a lot of eligible women have just come knocking on your door."

"Only you."

"See, that's my point exactly. I'm completely wrong for you. You don't even like people very much."

"I like people! What in the world gave you that crazy idea?"

"Everything in your apartment revolves around your work. You have computer equations written on the back of your jar of peanut butter, but no personal mementos."

"Do you make it a habit of insulting your employers?"

"It's not an insult. I'm just saying that we're very different people. And that's why I needed to draw up a schedule so that you wouldn't dump Juliet on me and then proceed to forget all about her."

"Trust me, I could never do that."

SAM COULD NOT BELIEVE how infuriating that woman was. She looked at him and decided she knew all about him. She didn't.

After dinner, he'd escaped to his office to work on his voice-activated daytimer. He'd pleasantly lost himself inside an improvement for several hours, until Anne had walked in to tell him that she was putting Juliet to bed, and did he want to say good-night?

The hell of it was that he knew she was in the room before she said a word. Nor had he heard a footstep or a peep out of Juliet. He'd been caught up in a particularly difficult part of the equation when he suddenly knew that Anne was in the room with him. What did that mean? Why did all of his senses go on alert whenever she was around?

And now he couldn't sleep.

Anne's brother, the famed Davis Logan she had spent much of dinner talking about, had arrived sometime after dinner. He was a very attractive young man with the same blond hair as Anne, a confident smile and an easy way about him, but Sam had noticed how carefully Anne had looked at him with her brother present and how her smile seemed more strained. Davis had helped them move the bed out of the guest bedroom into the other room. Wasn't that just like her? She was only going to be in his house for a week or two and yet she had to rearrange everything to her liking. It would have been easier for everyone if she'd taken the guest room, but she'd insisted the view was so much better from the other room.

All he knew was that she'd better not bring home any of her dates to her room. He'd break the guy's neck.

Now why was he thinking like that?

He wasn't going to become involved with a woman like Anne Logan. She was one hundred percent completely wrong for him…and absolutely gorgeous. The way her upper lip curved into a perfect cupid's bow, and the soft blush of rose that traveled across her cheekbones when she became excited, which was frequently—these traits were only distractions that meant nothing to him. She was far too pretty and family-oriented for a man like him. He would ignore whatever small, ridiculous attraction he felt for her.

He had just been without a woman for too long. It had been months since he'd spoken to any woman other than the ones he worked with. Maybe he shouldn't have broken up with Marianne. Except they hadn't really broken up; he'd just forgotten about her.

Work was the answer. It was reliable and challenging—more than any relationship could be for him. He could focus exclusively on his computer programs, give them everything he was capable of and they never failed him. Answers were possible. His imagination led and the capacity to create what he dreamed of followed. Take Diva for example. The miniature, voice-activated daytimer would be a boon to busy people's lives. Ellen and he had considered over a dozen offers before deciding to sell to Comput-Extra.

He was distracted because of the baby. Juliet had thrown him off stride and Anne was only exacerbating the problem. He liked being alone. The presence of the two strangers in his home was disturbing his sleep.

What he needed, since he couldn't sleep thinking about Anne so close by, was to go downstairs to his office and work for a couple of hours. Or maybe through the night. Maybe, if Ellen was going to be in Seattle for a while, he could convince Anne and Juliet to move into Ellen's apartment.

That wasn't a bad idea. He'd give some thought as to how he could present it to Anne, he decided, as he pulled on a pair of jeans and a T-shirt and then stepped out into the hallway. He didn't want to wake Anne or the baby unnecessarily, so he kept the lights off and walked soundlessly down the hallway in his bare feet. He left the door to his apartment ajar slightly, because it creaked whenever you shut it, and so he could hear if Anne needed him—if Juliet woke up and wouldn't stop crying or something like that. Right, maybe he could fool his computer into believing that story.

On the balls of his feet, he made his way down the steps to the first floor office of E^2. As he began to punch in the entry code, he saw that the green light was on—someone was already in the office, having deactivated the alarm. He looked again. The light was definitely green. Someone was inside.

Ellen was in Seattle, so it couldn't be her. Neither Susan nor Walter, the only two other employees of E² who knew the entry combination, would be working late on a Saturday night. In fact, he'd never known either of them to return to work late at night as he did. They had lives.

Should he race back upstairs and call the police or find out who the devil was stealing from him—and what the person wanted?

Sam knew it was his new program. By the time he got back upstairs, the burglar could be gone—with the information. He wasn't about to lose a year's work. Pushing the door open silently, he peered into the darkness but saw nothing in the front room other than the usual couch and two chairs and reception desk. He knew this floor plan blindfolded, so walking around the furniture in the dark was easy. Behind the receptionist's desk was the large work area with desks for himself, Ellen, Walter, Susan and Hal. Sometimes E² hired freelancers, but in general they kept their staff down to half a dozen, which was why they were able to share one large work space. Along with the computer terminals were one round table, and a couch and coffee table area. You could move around and work wherever you wished—or spend time reading or relaxing on the couch or overstuffed chairs. The last room in the house was the conference room for formal presentations and meetings.

He saw the beam of a small flashlight over by Ellen's desk. Clearly the burglar wasn't exactly where he would find the information he needed. That was good; that meant he hadn't found what he was looking for yet.

Crouching down, Sam used the lounging area furniture and then the computer desks for cover as he moved slowly through the room, keeping his presence unknown.

"Nothing," he heard a man's voice say. "There's nothing on the database—"

Sam raised his head slightly to see who was speaking when he felt something hit him hard on the head. Then everything went black.

"SAM, CAN YOU HEAR ME?"

Sam heard a loud banging in his head, a noise that, for once, wasn't the baby crying, and it was all his body was aware of. Then, he realized the person speaking was Anne, her tone soft and worried. He opened his eyes very carefully to see her lovely face above his.

She stroked his brow. "Thank God you're alive."

He realized his head was cradled on her lap and he smelled lavender and vanilla. "I like your perfume."

"What? Shh, don't say any more, you're hallucinating. You've got a huge lump on the back of your head."

He remembered going downstairs to work. "Somebody hit me, knocked me unconscious." He struggled to sit up, but Anne held him down with her soft, gentle, small hands on his massive shoulders. Because his head hurt worse than the morning after he'd celebrated finishing his doctorate in artificial intelligence, he let his head rest on her lap.

"Yes. I heard a noise, like a shout, and when I got out of bed to investigate, I saw someone, a shadow really, run out of the front door. You must have interrupted a burglary."

He closed his eyes and then opened them again. "My work. Someone was trying to steal my latest project." Over the years, he'd heard stories of high-tech thefts, but had never overly worried about it. The security system they'd installed on the building was first-rate, but then he remembered the green light—the burglar had known the entry code. "Someone knew the entry code," he said out loud, not meaning to, but his brain wasn't working well yet. That was the only reason he would have confided in Anne.

Anne paled. "Someone knew the code? But how… Can you sit up? Should I phone the police?"

Sam let her help him upright and move him to one of the overstuffed chairs. He sank into it gratefully, and touched the goose egg on the back of his head. It felt huge and ready to hatch.

"Do you want me to call the police?" Anne asked again.

If he'd been thinking more clearly, he would have thought it odd that she hadn't called them immediately, but then again, maybe she'd panicked. Still, Anne didn't look like the kind of woman who panicked. "No, no police. I don't want the publicity."

"You don't? Is what you're working on really valuable?"

"Ellen is going to sell Diva for a lot of money to ComputExtra. It's the deal she's working on out in Seattle."

Anne pleated the fold of her nightgown and he noticed she hadn't thrown a robe over it. It was pale pink with spaghetti straps and some kind of soft sheer material that floated around her and clung to all the right curves. His mouth went dry. "Water," he croaked. "Could I have some water?" He watched her glide away from him toward the coffee station and pull out a bottle of water from the minifridge. He couldn't keep his eyes off her every sexy curve as she walked back toward him and handed him the bottle. If he were Adam he would have taken the apple from her.

Anne brushed hair off her face and the movement stretched the bodice of her gown tight across her breasts. "Can you tell me what you're working on? What Diva is?"

Adam swallowed half the bottle of water, trying to quench the fire that was building. He was not going to touch her. "It's not a big secret, but I don't want any negative publicity, especially with Ellen finishing our negotiations with ComputExtra."

She nodded and sat across from him, still unaware of how aware he was of her and her state of undress. He, however, couldn't take it anymore—because of his weakened state. Otherwise, she wouldn't be affecting him like this. Hell, he hadn't been this randy as a sixteen-year-old. "Maybe we should go back upstairs," he suggested, his voice gruff. "I don't think we should leave Juliet alone."

"Of course." Anne jumped out of her chair. "How silly of me. I wasn't thinking. Here, you're still weak. Let me help you." With that, she tucked herself under his shoulder and wrapped both arms around his waist as she helped him make it across the office and back up the stairs to the apartment. Every step of the way, he called himself a fool but he didn't tell her to move away, either. Instead he let himself enjoy the feel of her body against his, her intoxicating scent of vanilla and lavender, the way her curls tickled his nose and her surprising strength. She steered them toward the nursery where Juliet was sleeping like a baby.

If he was another kind of man, he would thank his aunt Gwen for sending Anne Logan his way and take what he wanted. But she was only going to be in his house for a week or two, and then she'd be gone. He didn't want more of her imprinted on the house than was absolutely necessary. Normally he never noticed that he was alone, but he was afraid that after Anne was gone, he would.

It didn't matter that he was lonely because he wasn't. Well, sometimes he was, but he was used to it. Ellen and Gwen had been his lifesavers from the terrible home his parents had created. Ellen's parents, while horrific to each other, had loved her. They just hadn't really known what to do with her.

But Sam, with his oversized body and oversized brain? Growing up, it was like his parents couldn't love him—

every time they looked at him it was with shock and revulsion. Later in school, he'd learned he could beat up the other kids in his class, much older kids, when necessary, but it never won him any compatriots. And then much later, when because of his size girls flirted and teased him, he'd been out of his element. He was, after all, a fourteen-year-old boy being teased and tormented by seventeen-year-old girls. And he'd retreated totally into himself.

And those lessons still stuck with him.

Anne stopped by the makeshift crib, the light from the hallway illuminating Juliet's face. "Isn't she beautiful?"

"Yes," he answered, but when she looked at him, she saw he wasn't looking at the baby. He clenched his fists, keeping his hands to himself. He wasn't going to make the mistake of reaching out for her—he didn't want to know if she would let him.

Anne blushed and she looked down at herself, for the first time noticing her state of undress. "Oh, I was in such a rush…"

She moved to brush past him in the doorway and he couldn't resist. He stopped her with his hands on her shoulders, her bones and skin feeling so delicate under his large grip. "I don't—" she spoke to the floor and then looked up at him. He knew what she'd seen in his face: a need, a want, a desire unlike any he'd ever felt before in his life. "Sam—" she shook her head ever so slightly "—this is a terrible idea." But she didn't try to break free of him. Not even when he pulled her closer to him very slowly, giving her every opportunity to run for her life, because he'd never wanted to kiss a woman like he did now.

His kiss would tell her all that and more.

4

HE KISSED HER.

Annie was so sweet. With one of his big hands in her riot of luxurious blond curls, her familiar scent of vanilla and lavender enveloping him, he tilted her face so he could take complete possession of her mouth. He wanted to taste her, devour her. He wanted in so he ran his tongue in darting strokes over her lips. She parted her mouth under his assault. When he explored her mouth, she moaned.

He heard the sound and he pressed her more firmly against him, needing the feel of her skin, the length of her body against his. He curved his hand along her hip. She was all softness and warmth in his arms, sweetness and wonder against his mouth.

Never before had any woman tasted like this, felt like this. He was overcome with emotion. Not just sexual desire—although it was pounding through his body—but need. He needed her. He wanted to see passion for him in her eyes, but also to hear her laugh as he told her what had happened to him during the course of the day while they were apart. He wanted her to miss him when he wasn't there.

He angled his mouth over hers again, this time more gently and she was the one who pressed against him, her lips matching his hunger, his need. Yes, he wanted to shout like a conquering warrior. You are mine. With a growl he picked her up and started to step out of the nursery to his room. He wanted her in his bed tonight. He nuz-

Baby.com

zled her neck; her skin was so soft…like warm velvet. His flesh burned as he stroked the side of her breast.

Anne gasped and shifted within his arms. "Sam…I wasn't expecting… I want…You're so…" She pulled his head back up to hers and kissed him, hard, then broke it off. "Put me down, please."

Her words registered slowly, but when they did he looked at her. Her cheeks were tinged with rose, her lips swollen by his kisses but her eyes told him that a kiss was all they were going to share. The blue was like arctic water, as though to douse the fire between them. Which she had.

He stepped away. "Damn."

Anne blushed and hugged her arms over her aroused breasts in the sheer nightgown. He was too aware of her exposed body, reached for the spare blanket on the bed and passed it to her. "Wrap yourself up in this. It's cold."

She wrapped the baby blanket around herself, but continued to stare at her feet. He waited impatiently for her to say something, wanting her to confirm what he knew. That he was a great bear of a man who she wanted no dealings with. That she might have some animal attraction toward him but that he didn't fit into her plans for the kind of man she could love.

For one moment they'd shared something, but that was as far as it would go. The kiss had been wonderful and rather magical, but he wasn't going to repeat that mistake. Because it was a mistake for two people who saw the world completely differently.

Well, he hadn't been looking for love, had he? All he'd wanted was to take her to bed and bury himself into her sweetness because he hadn't had a woman in months. Who had he taken to Martin's wedding? Stephanie? He'd call her tomorrow and ask her out again. She'd been…interesting, he was sure of it. They'd had a nice time at the wedding; moreover, she hadn't gotten mad at him when he'd disappeared for an hour to work out an equation he'd thought might help Diva's logic abilities. The answer hadn't worked, but it had led him onto the path that would. Yes, he'd find Stephanie's number—Diva should have it—he'd call her up and ask her out. Then he wouldn't be coming on to the nanny the very first evening she spent in his home.

Finally, Anne looked up at him, squaring her shoulders under the ridiculous blanket. "I'm sorry." Her face said she was embarrassed and worried about what he was going to do next.

Clearly her employers didn't come on to her on a regular basis—or at least not on the first day together. He had to remember she was his employee. If she'd been working downstairs in E², frowning at a computer screen, the glare of the screen casting a green shadow on her face, he wouldn't have noticed the way her jeans clung to her backside or the T-shirt that showed off her slender arms. Yes, he'd still notice her but he wasn't going to do anything about it. "Don't be. I'm the one who mauled you. I wouldn't blame you if you didn't want to spend the night under my roof—your first night, for God's sake." He shook his head, amazed at his lack of self-control. Hadn't his whole life been about control? He'd learned to take what his prodigious intelligence offered him, to compartmentalize the hurts that came from what he couldn't have, and now all his barriers were being attacked by this woman wearing a blanket with baby bears all over it. "Your first night and I can't keep my hands off you. I'm sorry. It won't happen again. If you like, I'll sleep in Ellen's apartment until she returns. When she's back, she can move in with you down here."

"No, Sam, that's not what I want. I trust you. These things happen sometimes, two people alone together. Not that they happen to me all the time—or ever. But it can. I've been told. Tonight was because of what happened to you downstairs—the burglars. My God, I almost forgot about that. Should we call the police?"

"Take a breath."

"I'm rambling. Shoot. I always blither on like an idiot when I'm nervous. Not that I'm nervous for any particular reason. I mean, not because of you. Well, maybe because of you, because I have other reasons to worry, to be out of control..." Anne stopped and blushed. She hugged her arms more tightly around herself. "What about calling the police?"

"No, there's no need. The police won't find anything and will only keep us up for most of the night when we could use our sleep."

Anne nodded, looking down at her bare feet and biting her lip. Finally she took a deep breath. "I have a very firm rule about dating my employers. It only leads to difficulties."

"Do most of your male employers come on to you?" Sam was surprised by the edge in his voice.

"No, that's not it. Only once, really, and it was a mistake." She played with the ends of the blanket. "I'll only be here a couple of weeks and then both Juliet and I will be gone. Any involvement would be..."

"Pointless. You're looking for a husband."

"You do state your words very plainly. Yes, I want a husband and a family, but I also want to fall in love. You make what I want sound like a bad thing, like love is the worst thing that can happen to you."

"Love works better for some people more than others. All you need to remember is that I'm not the kind of man who wants a family."

Before Anne could agree with him, Sam left the makeshift nursery and escaped to his own room. He heard her make a sound behind him but he heard his own words echoing in his head. What kind of an idiot was he, saying something like that? Like he would want little Miss

Housewife to fall in love with him, have his babies and cook casseroles. She was exactly like Darlene and he'd wiggled out of that trap once.

That was it. He was attracted to Anne because she reminded him of Darlene Muesler. The sweet kindergarten teacher with the sparkling laugh and dancing brown eyes. They'd met at one of Martin's parties when he'd been trying to find someplace to put his oversize body. They had talked about mystery novels and she hadn't asked what he did for a living until their third date. All of his usual physical awkwardness had disappeared whenever he was around her. Even the fact that she told him she wanted a big family hadn't deterred his interest. In fact, he'd found himself buying her the biggest engagement ring Portland had to offer. Then they'd gone house shopping for a home big enough to accommodate all those children, and she'd asked if they could put a down payment on the biggest one.

She'd thrown her arms around him, screamed yes and asked if they could go to Paris for their honeymoon. Delighted and bemused by his good fortune, he'd agreed to everything.

Even when she flashed her ring to her friends and extrapolated on its carats and luster, he hadn't felt anything except proud. Like a lovesick fool, he hadn't suspected anything was amiss. Not even the fact that their infrequent lovemaking became next to nonexistent. Darlene had said their voluntary celibacy would make their wedding night more special. When he overheard Darlene bragging to the real estate agent how successful her fiancé was and the kind of life she planned to lead, he still wasn't suspicious.

He'd been a fool in love. So thrilled that Darlene wanted to build a life with him. A family. The thought had frightened him. Until Darlene, he'd never believed he could have any part of a life that included a woman like her. He'd been afraid, he admitted that to himself now, but all the time before Darlene, remaining alone had seemed cautionary and logical. With Darlene, he'd been willing to try.

But she had never loved him.

He wasn't about to make the same mistake with Anne Logan, no matter how beautiful and desirable she might be. Anne Logan could be the last single woman in Portland, Maine, and he still wasn't getting involved with her.

The only thing he needed to do was to remember not to kiss her.

ANNE RAN THE BLENDER and banged several pots together as she put them back in the cupboard. How could he sleep through such a racket? She looked at her watch again. Ten-fifteen. Where was Sam? Surely he couldn't still be asleep. Did the man dare have a good night's rest after kissing her like she'd never been kissed before, as if she'd never known what a lover's kiss could be? He'd wanted to make love to her, but he'd stopped. He'd stopped, insulted her and then left.

No, she was wrong about his actions—he'd wanted sex. He didn't want to love her; he'd made that very clear. For some reason, he didn't like her very much. She didn't know why, couldn't quite put her finger on how she knew, but there was something about her that disturbed him. She wasn't egocentric enough to think that everyone had to like her—although most people did—but she had barely been around long enough for Samuel Evans to discover a specific reason to have an aversion to her. It was more as if he disliked her on principle.

Well, it was Sunday morning and, no matter what he thought of her, he wasn't going to escape from his responsibilities to Juliet. She took a deep breath and marched to his bedroom. At the oak door, she faltered for a second and then raised her hand, rapped firmly and listened. Nothing. She knocked again. Still no answer. In her arms, Juliet waved at the door. Luckily the little girl hadn't complained about the noise Anne had made in the kitchen this morning making breakfast and an apple pie. Anne had never known any man who could sleep through the fragrance of a home baked pie. Instead Juliet had seemed amused by all of Anne's frantic activity.

She turned to the little girl. "What do you think, Juliet? Should we look inside?"

Juliet smiled a secretive smile, and Anne knew that Juliet knew she was dying to see inside Sam's bedroom. What if he slept nude and she saw all of his broad-muscled bare chest? She licked her dry lips. Sam Evans was so solid, a woman could attach herself to him and know she held firm to a massive tree with roots. No wind or storm would upset him. He could weather it all.

In the past, she had never found physical size, the sheer overwhelming masculinity of a man, to be of any importance. Before she met Sam that is. Last night all she'd been able to imagine was what it would be like to sleep next to Sam's massive body.

She twisted the knob and pushed open his door. The king-size wooden bed was neatly made, the brown duvet fluffed. His dresser was uncluttered; the open door to a wood console revealed a television. Sam, however, was gone.

"How did he escape?" she asked Juliet. The pair of them had been up since seven and she, a light sleeper, hadn't slept well at all. But still she hadn't heard Sam exit at any time during the early hours. He must have tiptoed past her bedroom. That would have been an interesting sight; she was sorry to have missed it.

The office, of course. He'd gone back to his office. Clearly he loved E^2 more than anything or anyone. Davis had told her that Sam Evans was a genius and a workaholic and now she was seeing it. She didn't understand people who substituted work for family, friends and a life. But then again, to be fair, maybe she had never felt passionate enough about any kind of work to imagine devoting every waking hour to it.

That wasn't the exact truth. She was passionate about her families—until Paul Stone. She adored helping guide young minds, showing them how to appreciate the world, how to have confidence, to believe that anything was possible. She hadn't been lying to Sam when she'd spoken about her own childhood. She'd seen from an early age how Betty Hendricks, the woman who had looked after her and Davis, had held her family together. Betty had made her and Davis's childhood a good one. She hated to think what her life would have been like without Betty.

Even when she'd been upset that her parents had no time for her, Betty had given her love and confidence. Anne knew her parents loved her, but they'd been so busy with their research—they were both medical doctors searching for the clues that would lead to a cancer gene—that they had seemed to forget they had children who needed parents. Instead the two of them had focused on their brilliant careers, and once she was older, she couldn't blame them. As co-directors of the Logan Institute, dedicated to genetic research, Doctors Logan and Logan made an excellent team, both searching for medical breakthroughs and willing to travel, speak at conferences and to media as well as join the Nobel prize-winning cocktail circuit to drum up the money so necessary for the institute's survival and growth. In so many ways, they were the perfect couple.

It wasn't their fault that their children could never be as important as each other.

Not that she blamed her parents, too much. They had been as good to her as they could be. The fact that they didn't, couldn't, invest the same kind of time and imagination into her childhood as they could into the institute was rooted in their character. When she was fourteen, she had spent months reading psychology texts, classifying the kinds of families all her friends had—and learning about her own parents. That's when she'd begun to forgive them. Most importantly, they had given her Betty. And set out the path for her own future.

Anne Logan had vowed she would never be her parents. When she had a family, her children and husband would be first.

Only recently had she begun to worry about her very excellent plans for the future. After all, she would soon be thirty and she had expected to be married with two children by now. Instead, as Sam had pointed out, she was still looking after other people's children.

"Come on, Juliet. We're going to go find Sam." Now that she wasn't waiting for Sam to emerge from his bedroom, she felt relieved. There was nothing more she hated than waiting. Planning and action were her forte.

She and Juliet skipped down the steps to the office. E² was an unusual name. She rather doubted that Sam had chosen it; he didn't seem to have much of a sense of flair. It was probably Ellen's choice. Anne was looking forward to meeting the famous cousin—the one woman Sam seemed to admire.

Just like last night, the door was open. When she'd gone looking for him after hearing a noise and seen his still body on the floor, she'd felt ill. With shaking hands, she'd tried for his pulse, and only when she'd felt the strong beat had her own heart joined in the rhythm. Still, the sight of such a powerful man unconscious and vulnerable had disturbed her more than she liked to admit.

This morning Sam was hunched over a computer screen. She couldn't help watching and appreciating the sheer masculinity of him. The phone rang and Sam reached for it. After he'd said hello and grinned in recognition, he noticed Anne and Juliet by the door and waved for them to come in.

"Ellen," he spoke into the phone. "Tell me about dinner

last night. Is the deal finished?" He frowned at her response. "What do you mean they're acting funny? How?" He listened. "Is someone else trying to sell to Comput-Extra? I thought no one else had their project as far along as ours." He listened to her words again, keystroking at the same time. Anne walked farther into the room and couldn't help but look over Sam's shoulder. He'd opened a new file and was typing what Ellen was telling him along with questions and possibilities.

She closed her mouth. Sam was carrying on a conversation, recording it and analyzing possibilities simultaneously. He had typed: *Who else working on voice-activated daytimer? Ellen, dinner with ComputExtra, bad vibes.* Her lips twitched at his phrasing. More and more, she was looking forward to meeting Ellen, since he valued her opinion. Davis hadn't said much about Sam's partner, except that they shared the Victorian house. She knew there was another apartment on the top floor of the building and felt a sudden flare of envy. Envious of his good relationship with his cousin? That was ridiculous because Sam didn't like her very much and he was all wrong for her. All they had was chemistry, and chemistry was not a relationship.

When Sam hung up the phone he glared at the computer screen. Anne waited but Juliet didn't have her patience. The baby let out a cry.

Sam jumped. "I forgot you were here."

"Yes. Juliet wants you." The baby flailed around with her arms reaching for Sam.

He reached for the little girl absentmindedly. Juliet managed to grasp his hair and pulled determinedly. Sam grimaced and gently unclasped her grasp. "You're strong for such a pretty little thing."

"Don't stereotype her yet. She's only a few months old. She'll learn all about our male dominated society and female expectations soon enough."

Sam raised the little girl to his face level and spoke softly as Juliet studied him intently. "I'm sure that through your nurturing and by your example in the advanced female role of child caregiver, she'll become an astronaut." Juliet opened her mouth and copied Sam's lip actions as a string of drool dribbled onto his shirt.

Anne bit her lip to stop herself from laughing. "I wish I had more time with Juliet. I would show her the full range of possibilities for women."

He grabbed a tissue, wiped the drool off his shirt and sat Juliet on his lap. "Did you want something?"

"I wanted to know what your plans for the day were."

"I'm going to do what I'm doing right now—work. I have a few ideas for improvements on the program Ellen is selling that still need to be worked out. If I can finish in the next couple of weeks, Ellen will have an updated program to market to ComputExtra."

"It's Sunday."

"Yes. Ellen's meeting with ComputExtra tomorrow and she thinks she'll be there for most of the week feeling out the company. If I stay at this I could have the upgrade ready to run before she returns."

"You're forgetting about Juliet."

He held two fingers in front of her face and Juliet grabbed for them. He laughed. "That is impossible. I seem to be more aware of Juliet than I have ever been aware of anyone."

"I was hired to help take care of her, not to become her primary care provider. Juliet is your responsibility."

"I never asked for Juliet."

"No, but your aunt clearly thinks you need her."

He frowned. "My aunt Gwen is a meddler. But this time she's gone too far and overreacted. There is nothing wrong with my life. And certainly nothing that a baby can cure. I don't want a baby."

Anne wondered about that. Exactly what was the woman who had hired her trying to accomplish? She had seemed like such a polished successful businesswoman who was merely handling a detail that her overworked nephew would be too overwhelmed to handle. Juliet gave another little cry, pulling their attention back to her. Satisfied she had them both with her, she gurgled.

"Juliet needs some fresh air, as do I. I suggest we go to the park for a walk."

"A walk?"

"Yes. One foot in front of the other. Fresh air. Other people also outside. Maybe playing with dogs and Frisbees. Round plastic things you throw."

"You can go without me."

"No," Anne said very definitely, treating him as firmly as she used to treat Patrick Stone, aged seven. "We're going to the park, together. Just like a family."

JUST LIKE A FAMILY. He couldn't get the words out of his head. Anne Logan had done more to disturb him in less than twenty-four hours than Conrad Blackenburg, the schoolyard bully had, during Sam's entire fourth-grade year.

No matter what the temptation, he wasn't going to kiss her again. All he had to do was remember that she would be gone in a week at the most and then his life would return to normal.

So then why was he going for a walk in the park with Anne and the baby when his *real* baby—his daily calendar program—needed him? A few hours off wouldn't hurt, he rationalized. He'd stay up late tonight and work on his project. He'd show Miss Supernanny that he could be as caring as the next guy, if he wanted. It was just that usually he didn't want.

He liked being alone. The only real family he wanted was Ellen. And occasional visits from Aunt Gwen and Uncle Theodore. Chicago was only a two-hour plane ride away, but E² kept Sam too busy for many visits.

Shutting off the computer, he suddenly remembered a story his aunt had told him about how she had met Theodore. Something to do with her being too busy for a husband because of her career. She had been one of the trailblazing feminists in the sixties, leading the charge up the corporate advertising ladder. Gwendolyn Parker had handled only the biggest accounts and made vice president of her Manhattan advertising firm while most women were breast-feeding their second baby.

She'd loved those days, she'd told him and Ellen. Moreover, she had never really known anything was missing. She'd dated a variety of men, but they hadn't been interested in anything serious and neither was she. Her mother had nagged her to find a husband, to have children, much like Aunt Gwen nagged him and Ellen. And then her mother had taken action.

Aunt Gwen had never been very clear on the specifics, but her mother had played matchmaker between her and Theodore. Sam found out that, not only had the determined mother invited the two of them to a Vermont hideaway for Christmas, but had cut off the phone service and transportation, leaving them isolated for seven days. On the eighth day, they had found a justice of the peace and gotten married. After the honeymoon, Gwen continued her successful career, although she no longer devoted eighteen-hour days to it. Instead Theodore and Gwen devoted themselves to each other.

While they'd never had children, or very much wanted them, Gwen said, she loved her summers looking after Ellen and Sam. Just as they had loved their summers with her. Both of the lost children escaping the misery of their lives with their real families.

How ironic that Gwen should now send a baby to him to try to fix his life. What exactly did she think was going to happen? Did she expect him to fall for Juliet's big brown eyes and dark curly lashes and rosebud lips. The way she tried to reach for whatever wasn't in her grasp, or the way she snuggled up to him when he sat at the computer keyboard and seemed to hang on to his every word as he explained mathematical problems and solutions to her?

Perhaps Aunt Gwen was regretting never having any children and wanted Sam to have children for her to grandmother.

No, that couldn't possibly be it. If Gwen wanted to be a grandmother, surely Ellen was the much more likely candidate. Ellen had even been showing those worrisome signs that something wasn't right with her, that in some way she was dissatisfied with her life.

The entire thinking process was illogical. Nothing and no one was going to change his life unless he wanted it changed. He was happy. Happy, dammit.

He grabbed his black leather jacket and hurried down the stairs to the porch where Anne Logan was waiting with Juliet.

The last thing in the world he wanted in his life was either a woman or a baby.

And certainly not a wife and daughter!

5

NOW WHAT HAD SHE DONE to make him scowl as if she'd taken away his favorite toy and insisted he had to finish his plateful of peas?

Anne reminded herself that Sam Evans wasn't her problem—even if he could kiss better than any man had a right to. Clearly she was having a bad reaction to men. Once she'd been so sure of her instincts, but now she doubted herself. First, Paul Stone. Now, Samuel F. Evans. What did the *F* stand for? Probably fiendishly handsome. Capable of turning women into fools for love.

Anne Logan wasn't about to be made into a fool for love. Moreover, Samuel F. Evans did not match her type. He was a workaholic whose only real love was his inventions. Of course, he did care for Ellen—and Aunt Gwen, or else he would never have agreed to the ridiculous situation his aunt had forced him into. Sam wasn't really a man who could be forced. Power and confidence exuded from him and not just because of his size.

Sam did what he thought was right. At this time, doing right meant looking after Juliet and tolerating Anne.

Anne shook her head. Never before had she felt that she didn't know what to do. That she'd just like to daydream about Sam and her…. No. She was going to pull herself together. Tonight she'd lock herself in her bedroom and draw up a list of the reasons why Sam was the wrong man for her. She could already picture the list, the column full of negatives long and bold—but would it be enough to block out how well he could kiss?

She'd dated handsome men before, but never a man whose presence took up all the space around them. She'd barely spent a day with him, yet she was more aware of Sam than any other person she could remember meeting.

Maybe that was because she had never met a genius before. Part of his aura came from Sam's confidence in his own abilities. His mind was always racing ahead, able to see what a person like her couldn't even begin to imagine. She could plan a superb dinner party and see the potential in an old piece of furniture, but she couldn't envision the future as Sam did.

Pleased with the logic of her argument, she smiled, and then remembered Sam's potent sexual appeal. Genius or not, no one had ever claimed that Albert Einstein was hot, while every hormone in her body got all squishy and alive every time Sam came within twenty feet of her.

Well then, she was back to her list. And to staying at least twenty feet away whenever possible. Unfortunately Sam's bedroom was much closer than twenty feet.

She was in big, big trouble.

Sam's long strides ate up the path that wound along the park. A pair of inline skaters whizzed past them as Anne had to race to keep up with Sam. To her surprise, none of the women they passed along the path had taken a second look at Sam. In fact, she could have sworn that one woman, after looking at Sam, kept her gaze fixed straight ahead so that she wouldn't have to acknowledge him. "Slow down," she called out as he hurried away from her. Or had he simply forgotten about her? He looked back over his shoulder with surprise and adjusted his pace.

Great, Anne thought. Here she was analyzing all her reactions to him, realizing the need for a safety zone, and he had forgotten she existed. She touched his arm lightly, wishing he wouldn't look so ruggedly handsome in his well-worn jeans and leather jacket. He stopped and looked at her. Bad mistake, as she remembered what it felt like to be held in his arms. She forgot what she was going to say, but that had never stopped her before. "It's a beautiful day, but it's like you want to rush through it. We don't have to be anywhere for hours." She wanted to tell him to relax, to loosen the tensions in his shoulders, but she didn't dare. "Davis said he might pull out his skates and join us later on."

Sam studied her carefully and she wondered what he was looking for. "You and your brother spend a lot of time together?"

"Not really. He was only twelve when I went to college, and then I worked in Seattle, Chicago and New York while Davis went to university in California and then stayed to work there as well."

"Why did he decide to move to Portland?"

"It was because of a girl, I think." She thought back to their infrequent conversations and how he used to talk about Joy. Shortly after he moved to Portland, he never mentioned Joy again. "He never said anything directly to me, but I know my brother. If he was in love with a girl, he'd move out here to join her."

"Like his sister."

"We're both romantics at heart." She sighed and brushed away hair that the wind had blown into her face. "I just wish Davis was a little more..."

"Practical?"

"Yes. You saw it right away, didn't you? He's always dreaming of the big idea he's going to have instead of..."

"Working on it?" he asked gently.

"Yes. It's hard sometimes, seeing your brother as he really is. I still think of him as my little brother who needs my protection. I wish he was more like you."

Sam stopped moving and Anne bumped into him. "You think he should be more like me? How?"

His eyes blazed at her as he waited for her answer. She

licked her dry lips wondering what it was he wanted her to say. "You're focused and driven—a practical dreamer."

His face relaxed. "A practical dreamer. You have an odd way of saying things, Anne Logan." He began to walk again.

She grabbed his arm. "It's true. Everything you and your cousin have created has come out of your dreams. You're not afraid to take risks but you also understand how to get it done. You don't just dream, you make it happen."

"A lot of people would say that Ellen is the one who makes sure it gets done."

Anne shook her head. "No, it's the two of you together."

"You seem to know me better than many of my friends." He reached out and cupped her face, looking intently at her. In his eyes, she saw his sudden awareness of his touch on her skin and he lowered his mouth.

Anne broke away from him and fussed through the baby bag she had slung over her shoulder. She had to remember getting involved with Sam was a mistake. A big one. A colossal-sized one. Her brief dalliance with Paul Stone had been humiliating, but it hadn't left her brokenhearted. She was afraid that Sam might.

No matter how much she wanted him to kiss her, no matter how much she wanted to kiss him, she wasn't going to.

When she dared to look up, Sam was looking away from her toward Fore River. "We should start walking again. We can't keep Juliet out that long before she needs a diaper change. I left a lot of work back at the office. Plus, I have several ideas about my computer program that I want to test out today. I need to update my daily calendar."

Anne tapped the bag she had slung over her shoulder. "I have enough supplies to keep Juliet happy throughout the morning. Today is Sunday—surely you can plan your schedule later. I thought I was the one who was obsessive about schedules and clocks—I learned a long time ago, if you plan your day properly you can fit so much into it— but you're even worse than me. Aren't you supposed to be an absentminded genius who works whenever the muses strike him?" She couldn't stop her mouth and wondered why she wanted Sam with her. It would be better if she let him get back to work while she and Juliet waited for Davis. "Is there a muse for computer science? I guess not. But surely you could appropriate the one for mathematics." She tilted her head in thought. "Or maybe music. It seems like you can hear something the rest of us can't." She stopped because he was looking at her funny. She recognized the look. It often appeared when she rambled, which unfortunately, was far too often. "I'm talking too much. Sorry."

He stared at her out of those dark brown eyes, and she could see him working back through her conversation to the point he wanted. "Not my personal calendar. I've created a computer model."

"But there are lots of computer calendars. Patrick Stone, he was seven, showed me his and tried to get me to use one myself."

"Did you?"

"No. It was horrible. I liked the ease of pencil and paper and being able to carry it with me at all times and make changes simply. It's much simpler to cross out an appointment and write over it than to remember it, go home, turn on your computer, access the right file and then keystroke in the changes." She shrugged. "I tried it several times, and deleted all the appointments I'd scheduled for a month. That's when I returned to my handy old-fashioned paper calendar."

Sam nodded as if she'd told him exactly what he wanted to hear. "Diva is voice-activated and portable."

"Portable? How big is it?"

"About the size of an index card—and it doesn't weigh much more. Smaller than most old-fashioned paper calendars."

"And it's voice-activated?" She was beginning to understand why Davis was so in awe of Sam's success.

Sam shifted Juliet in his arms and she reached out to touch his face. He smiled and his voice grew lighter. "Not only does Diva respond to your voice commands but she can talk back to you, warning of scheduling conflicts and providing verbal reminders of appointments and deadlines."

Anne was all caught up in admiring how his face had changed, how he had looked at Juliet with affection, and she wished he would look at her the same way. Oh, no, she wasn't going there. She didn't want him to kiss her again, she reminded herself. "Diva?" she asked him instead.

"An acronym for Digitally Initiated Voice Action. Diva. Plus, she really does have the attitude of a prima donna when you're not listening to her."

"That's amazing." Anne used both hands to pull back the hair the wind was whipping around her face and secured it in a knot on the top of her head. Sam's gaze followed her actions and a curious expression crossed his face, but then Juliet waved a hand at him, pulling his attention back to her.

Careful, Anne told herself again. She was becoming jealous of Juliet.

Sam gave Juliet a finger to hold on to. "Diva is the program Ellen is selling to ComputExtra. I realize that every new technological breakthrough is heralded as the next big thing, but Diva really will revolutionize how an ordinary person can store and organize all the information we need. For example, if your son has a doctor's appointment at three o'clock, Diva will pinpoint where you are that afternoon, calculate the amount of time required to travel to the doctor's office and then remind you at the appropriate time to leave for the appointment."

"Wow. You could put people like me out of work."

"I doubt that. You'd be too busy meddling to let Diva take your place."

"You know me pretty well." She smiled at him and he smiled back. The sun shone off his black hair and the firm line of his mouth. His very kissable mouth. "My brother will be so impressed. Whenever he explains one of the projects he's working on, I never understand what he wants to accomplish. But Diva is so obvious and, well, so perfect. Is it a secret? Can I tell Davis about it?"

"Diva's existence isn't a secret. When Ellen began shopping around the technology the word spread quickly."

"So most people in the computer industry know about Diva? That's funny, Davis never mentioned it and he usually likes to tell me what's coming up that is going to revolutionize my life. He is enthusiastic about technology. But if you're still working on Diva, how can Ellen be selling it to ComputExtra?"

"I'm working on modifications for Diva II."

Anne laughed. "Diva's not even on the market yet and already you're developing an upgrade. You computer guys do seem intent on ruling the world—or at least having us sell it to you!"

Sam smiled again. "Diva II will contain more complete information including medical and financial records."

"A big brother Diva?"

"One you control. Let's say you take Juliet away on a trip and she gets sick and you end up in a hospital emergency room in the middle of the night. If you have Diva II, the hospital will be able to access her medical history."

"That's fantastic. It really would be information at our fingertips." What Sam was telling her about Diva was amazing—but now she had a new worry. "But what about the burglary last night? The thief broke into your office.

Do you think he was after your computer programs? I thought someone had broken into the bottom floor looking for cash or televisions or whatever..." She shivered.

"It's possible, especially since there were two men."

"Two men?"

"Yes, I entered the office while they were still inside. One of them was searching through the desks, trying to access my computer files. It sounded like he hadn't gotten anything when the second man hit me over the head."

"Two men. That sounds almost...professional."

"Yes. And the entry code to my office had been used."

"They had the code to get into your office?" Anne didn't know whether she considered that good or not. "Shouldn't you have phoned the police?"

"I doubt there is much the police can do. And it could have been a simple burglary. I didn't want to scare up undo alarm, especially while Ellen is in Seattle finalizing our deal with ComputExtra."

"What will ComputExtra do with Diva?"

"Our company, Ellen's and mine, is small. We like to keep it that way. We don't have the capacity to manufacture or sell a program like Diva. ComputExtra will buy it from us for a lot of money and then use their expertise to get it to market."

"What if someone else came out with a program like Diva?"

"It all depends on the timing and what the competing program can do. If a competitor comes out with a similar program months after Diva, then we've gained all the benefits of being first in the marketplace and the publicity surrounding our launch."

"If the program comes out at the same time?"

"It shouldn't happen. I haven't heard of anyone else who's as close as I am to voice-activated response on a miniature scale." Juliet gave a cry and he loosened his tense shoulders. "Except, of course, for little Miss Juliet here." He tickled Juliet under her chin and she gazed adoringly at him. "It's just that...it shouldn't be happening."

"And if ComputExtra hears rumors about a competing system...?"

"If it exists, our price will go down. ComputExtra will be rushing to try to get Diva into the marketplace first."

"Would it be so bad if you lost the money?"

"It's not for the money. Or even for the thrill of being first, although I do like to win. I don't like having my work stolen."

"Of course not. You're a man who's used to making his own way."

"For a long time."

They walked in silence for a few minutes as Anne considered what Sam had told her. Sam was the kind of man Davis dreamed of being. Clearly Sam was a lot smarter than Davis and perhaps willing to work harder. As much as she loved her brother, and would do anything for him, Davis was always looking for the shortcut. Dreaming of striking it rich. She hated to admit it, since he was her brother, but Davis was more of a dreamer than a doer.

Maybe she could invite Davis over for dinner one night and he and Sam could become friends. But when Davis had dropped off her suitcases last night he hadn't shown any indication of a desire to linger. In fact, he'd been in a downright hurry to leave, telling her she didn't need to walk him out the front door.

Thinking about her brother always gave her a slight headache and she rubbed her temples.

"Is something wrong?" Sam asked.

"No, nothing. I was just thinking—Davis!"

"Hey." Davis skated to a stop in front of them, looking casually athletic in a University of California sweatshirt and shorts, despite the chilly November weather. He grinned an easygoing smile at the three of them.

"You're going to freeze."

Davis kissed her on the cheek. "You're as bad as Betty. Trust me, maintaining my balance on these skates while the teenagers whip past me is keeping me warm. Nice to see you again." He nodded to Sam. "I see Anne has you enjoying the park with Juliet."

What was that funny edge to Davis's voice, as if he were taunting Sam about being under her thumb?

"I'm enjoying myself," Sam answered. "Anne said you might be joining us. She does seem good at scheduling our lives."

Davis's cheeks flushed. "She is at that. Listen, Anne, can I borrow your Swiss army knife? I've got these laces tangled up in a knot and I want to cut them loose." She dug through Juliet's diaper bag and pulled out the multipurpose knife and handed it to her brother. "Always prepared," she said to Sam, "just like the Boy Scouts."

Davis worked loose the knot, retied his skates and handed the knife back to Anne. "I'm sorry but I agreed to meet some friends down at the Old Port Exchange later on tonight so I can't stay."

Anne was disappointed. Despite the fact that she had moved to Portland for a few weeks in order to spend some time with Davis, she had barely seen him. He'd been too busy wrapped up with his own computer project, promising to make time for her as soon as he'd finished. But then he had encouraged her to take the job with Sam Evans, suggesting it was better than her sitting around his apartment waiting for him. Now, for the first time, she wondered if Davis had wanted to get rid of her. It was his way. In the few days she'd been with him, he'd insisted she shouldn't answer his phone as he was screening all of his calls. Could he be screening her out of his life, too? She looked at her brother with new eyes.

He was holding Juliet in his arms and the little girl seemed delighted with him. Anne realized she was being ridiculous in her imaginings. Trying to keep a tight rein on her libido while around Sam was making her think weirdly.

Davis handed Juliet back to Sam. "I'm sorry to rush but I have some work I need to finish before I meet my friends. Anne, I think you picked up one of my computer disks."

"Oh, I don't think so, Davis. I would have noticed. I'm very careful about that."

"Well, I've looked all over my place and it's not there. Can I look at your papers? It's possible that I'm the one who left the disk with your stuff—I remember looking through your retirement investments as you asked me to."

"Of course. I'll go through them tonight," she promised.

"I promised to show the program I was working on to these guys...they're kind of important...they might be willing to invest."

He put on his little-boy-pleading face and Anne couldn't resist. "All right, I'll come back with you—"

"No need to ruin your nice day. If you'll just give me your key, I'll let myself in and leave it in your bedroom— the door will automatically lock behind me when I leave."

"Go ahead," Sam suggested as Juliet struggled within his arms. "I don't want to be left alone with Juliet, it seems like she's getting fussy."

Anne handed over the key and turned to the baby who was getting cranky at being ignored. Juliet came happily into Anne's arms and rubbed her tiny face against the fleece of Anne's jacket.

"I think she likes the way you smell, too," Sam said, standing far too close to her.

She took a step back. "What?"

"Lavender and vanilla. It's a nice combination."

Surprised he should notice, she was about to tell him so when a man dressed in running shorts and a T-shirt did a double take and then headed back to them.

"Sam Evans, is that you?"

"Simon." Sam shook hands with the man. "You weren't at Martin's wedding."

"No, I was on the coast meeting with the big guys. I always thought Martin had a thing for your cousin."

"He did, but she wasn't interested. And that was over three years ago. Once he started dating Cynthia we all knew he was a goner. They seemed very happy at the wedding."

"Yeah, I took them out for a celebratory dinner a couple of weeks ago since I knew I wasn't going to be able to make the wedding. But what about you? I never heard a word about you tying the knot. It's hard to imagine Sam Evans settled down."

"What are you talking about?"

"I think he means me and Juliet," Anne said to the very confused Sam. She held out her hand to the handsome, blond, muscled runner. His sky-blue eyes swept over her appreciatively and she returned his infectious smile. "I'm Anne Logan, I'm the nanny and this is Juliet."

He took her hand in a firm grasp. "Simon Kensington. You're the nanny? None of my friends have such a good-looking nanny. If I'd known, I'd have begged, borrowed or stolen a baby to hire you for myself."

His line was outrageous but the warmth in his blue eyes and easy laugh made her join in. "If you find yourself a baby, I might just rush right over. But only if the baby is very, very cute."

"All babies are cute."

"A man who loves babies is a man after my own heart."

"Only if Sam hasn't already won it." Unbelievably Simon raised her hand to his lips and kissed it, his mouth warm against her skin, while Sam glared at him.

"Let go of my nanny."

Simon kept her hand in his and Anne liked his touch. He looked at Sam. "When did you have a baby?"

Sam raised his gaze from their clasped hands. "Juliet

isn't mine. I'm just looking after her for a few days. Annie is part of the package deal."

Anne raised her eyebrows at the diminutive of her name. Simon Kensington might be just the distraction she needed to keep herself away from Sam. "Are you a friend of Sam or Ellen?"

"Both, I think. Sam and I meet for a poker game every once in a while. In Portland, when you're in the same kind of business, you can't help but run into each other fairly regularly. Although, if I had known such a beautiful woman was around, I would have made a point to visit Sam."

"I only moved in yesterday."

"Then perhaps I'm not too late. I'd love to show you around our fair city sometime. Perhaps dinner later this week?"

She couldn't resist his appeal. "That would be lovely."

"You'll be busy with Juliet." Sam glared at her, his eyes dark.

"I have Thursday and Friday evenings free as per our arrangement." She felt pleased at the way his face darkened as she turned to Simon. "I explained to Sam they're preferred nights for dating."

"And catching a husband," he muttered.

Eyes flashing, she turned her sweetest smile on him. "I'm honest about what I want, and I'm not afraid to go after it. I don't hide away behind my computer screen, avoiding people, with only machines for friends." Anne bit her lips to stop herself from saying any more harsh words to Sam. What was it about the man that brought out the worst in her? Or the best, considering she only told him the truth.

With other people, despite her runaway mouth, she had some control. She learned to temper her words. But with Sam she just flat out said what she thought.

Simon's smile only wavered a little as he took in their

exchange. Then he turned it on with 100-watt intensity and punched Sam in the arm. "She's right. You do spend most of your days working."

"I enjoy working."

"You mean you get tired of people quickly. Why I've seen Sam tune out the conversation at a party if he finds it dull and retreat into his own world. But then again, even those of us who are no slouch in the brains department have to admit he's brilliant, so I guess we have to forgive Sam his eccentricities." Simon grinned. "Even if it means rearranging the pickle tray."

Anne laughed. "He did what?"

"It was at my Christmas party. Sam got some bright idea into his head and the next thing I knew he was busy rearranging the buffet table, using pickle slices and toothpicks as binary code."

Sam spoke for the first time. "I realized how to make Diva more voice-friendly. How she could recognize English with different accents."

"Everyone knows about Diva?" Anne asked, wondering why Davis had never mentioned it. He'd probably thought she wouldn't be interested.

"Of course, and we're all jealous. I tried to get Sam to sell Diva to my company, but he wanted to play with the big boys."

"Ellen and I looked at your offer carefully, but ComputExtra was offering much more in the market share it could penetrate and R&D money for future developments. Competitors will be in the market with cheap knockoff models only months after the launch so we needed to ensure E²'s future."

Simon held up his hands. "Hey, I understand. If I were in your shoes I would have made the same decision. I just wish Kensington Enterprises didn't always come in second to you." He turned to Anne. "But perhaps I won't be coming in second when it comes to winning the fair maiden's attentions."

"Anne and I are not involved. Nor are we interested in being involved." Sam crossed his arms over his chest.

Simon stared from Sam's glowering visage back to Anne. She couldn't help the smile that quirked her lips at Simon's blatant flattery and Sam's dour response. If she didn't know better, she'd say the man was jealous. Hah! He'd only be jealous of any competition because he was used to winning, not because he wanted her for himself. Why did that thought depress her?

"Let's make our date for Friday, then. I look forward to it." Simon grasped her hand again, and with a wave to Sam, resumed his jog. Anne admired his long-limbed stride and then returned to their walk in the opposite direction. "There, now, Juliet. Wasn't that a nice man? You can learn from him how men should behave toward women."

"Like a foppish idiot?"

"Like a gentleman," she corrected. "I'm looking forward to our date very much."

"You forgot to check out his bankbook before you agreed to see him." His voice was flat and Anne wondered who had wanted Sam for his money.

She quickened her pace to keep up with him. "My first priority for my future husband is that I'm in love with him. Simon Kensington seems very nice."

"You were attracted to him."

"Of course. He's a good-looking man."

He stopped and studied her. "But were *you* attracted to *him*?"

"Yes."

Anne had to race to catch up to Sam's quick strides. Juliet let out a little cry at her bumpy ride. Anne put her hand on Sam's arm, but quickly pulled it back.

Sam stopped dead still. "Is Juliet okay? Here, let me

hold her for a while." Juliet went into his big arms happily, wrapping her fingers around his thumb.

"Coo," she said to him.

"What?" He looked at Anne in puzzlement. "What did she say?"

"She didn't say anything. She's just making noise. Babies this young don't talk."

"She said 'coo.' I knew she was a smart little girl. Brilliant probably."

Anne wondered what it would be like to be the woman who captured Sam's heart as totally as Juliet had. She cleared her throat, wondering if she dared tell him that although she might find Simon attractive, she found Sam pretty well irresistible.

He looked up, his face blank. "Simon is a good man. He would probably make a great husband. He's responsible, successful, athletic. He's not afraid of hard work but he's not a workaholic, either."

"We're just going on a date," she protested, feeling the matter grow beyond her control. "A date doesn't mean we're getting married."

"You might marry him," Sam insisted.

"Well, yes, it's possible...but nothing's guaranteed."

"No, but it would be a good thing." Sam, holding Juliet, began to walk away from her.

Anne let him go, wondering what was wrong with her—and with Sam Evans. He should be trying to convince her not to date Simon Kensington. Dammit, he should be trying to kiss her.

Instead he seemed to be willing to forget all about her.

6

SAM MOVED THE CURSOR across the computer screen and entered the meeting time and location into Diva's files.

"Scheduling conflict. Please choose another time slot."

Diva's dulcet, slightly metallic, tone grated him, as did the fact that she was making a mistake. With Ellen in Seattle selling the prototype, he hoped there wasn't a bug in the program. Selling a defective computer program that promised as much as Diva did would damage E^2's reputation beyond repair. "What do you mean impossible? I want my meeting when I scheduled it."

"You have a Priority One meeting already in that time slot. Please pick another time slot."

Priority One was his innovation. It meant a very important engagement, one that took priority over all others. Other conferences were to be scheduled around the Priority One.

Diva really was beginning to annoy him. As were all women recently, including Ellen. When they had spoken on Monday afternoon, she'd told him the negotiations were proceeding as expected. She'd added, though, that she still thought the men negotiating across the table from her believed they were holding a trump card. The more the negotiations went on, the more nervous they made her, and Ellen didn't flinch easily.

He had thoroughly questioned her, and Ellen had shared all of her impressions with him. Neither of them held back—that was how they worked. They trusted each other absolutely. But while Ellen had a keen, analytical mind and could process vast quantities of information quickly, she also believed in and trusted her woman's intuition. Sam would have liked to have scoffed at the idea, but her intuition had been right too often. He wished he knew how intuition worked so he could gift it to one of his computers, but despite his study of the subject, he'd only become more confused. In this situation, the only thing he knew definitely was that he would never give Diva any more human characteristics; she was female enough already.

Just as Ellen was readying to end their conversation, he'd told her about Juliet and Anne. Rather than laughing as he'd expected, she'd been quiet for a moment and then grilled him about Anne. He'd found himself describing how natural and maternal she was with Juliet, how infuriating she'd been when she'd insisted he stop working and go for a walk in the park with them, and how she was making his apartment different.

"Different how?"

"Just different. She keeps moving small things around. Like that shelf that used to be next to the TV in the living room. She moved it across the room, angling it into a corner and then put Aunt Gwen's painting on top of it."

"The painting Gwen did of the house?"

"Yes."

"And...?"

"And it looks good there," he'd admitted.

"It sounds like Anne is doing more than just taking care of Juliet."

"Now you, my dear cousin, are doing it, too."

"What?"

"Matchmaking. There is nothing between Anne and myself." The kiss had been an aberration. After all, he'd been hit on the head and lost consciousness. A man in such a weakened state couldn't be expected to resist the lures of a seductress like Anne Logan.

Anne Logan a seductress?

He thought of the way she'd looked this morning with her hair pulled back in a ponytail, but with a few strands curling loose around her face, the knee-length, straight, flowered skirt in baby-blue and matching short-sleeved sweater. She was soft and feminine and positively maternal as she both played with Juliet and made him breakfast.

The picture had been so sweet that he had swallowed a lump in his throat. He'd ruthlessly quashed the feelings that Anne had called up from deep within him, reminding himself that he didn't fit into the pretty picture Anne and Juliet made. It wasn't only because of his oversized body and awkwardness around people, but because of his inability to love freely and completely.

Instead, he'd focused on his desire for Anne. He'd wanted to pull her down on the kitchen floor and devour her.

She was a temptress, all right. He just needed to keep reminding himself that Anne Logan was not the kind of woman he liked. Ever since Darlene, he'd made sure that he dated women who were too involved with themselves to tempt him into falling in love. He chose women who couldn't hurt him, who wouldn't touch his heart.

Unlike Anne.

He wasn't going to be rejected again.

"There's nothing between Anne and myself. She's just looking after Juliet."

Ellen made a funny sound over the phone but then her voice softened. "It sounds like Juliet has stolen your heart. I can't wait to meet her. I wish I could leave and come home." She sighed. "But these negotiations just feel all wrong. Have you had any more trouble since the break-in?"

"No. Nothing else has happened. It was probably an overreaction on my part—maybe the pair weren't after Diva."

"You heard them looking for something in the computer system," she reminded him.

"Yes, but I'd also spent a sleepless previous night looking after Juliet."

"Maybe you're right. But I've never known you to be distracted."

"I've never had a baby in the house before."

"Tell me about her. Juliet," she clarified when Sam remained silent.

"She's very sweet but she's just a baby. In a few days she'll be gone and a week after that I'll have forgotten all about her. You know what I'm like." He was a man who preferred being alone. Juliet was only a minor and temporary complication in his life. Anne was…a distraction. The only reason he had tossed and turned last night as he relived their kiss was that he was under a lot of stress. He was worried about Diva and the break-in, worried about the possible connection and Ellen's troubles with the negotiations.

"I know exactly what you're like Sam Evans, so don't try to pretend with me. I could kill that Darlene Muesler for what she did to you."

He gripped the receiver tightly. "Darlene didn't love me. I shouldn't have fooled myself into believing anything else."

"She was the fool," Ellen said hotly, always ready to come to his defense. Perhaps Aunt Gwen was right that he and Ellen relied on each other too much, to the point of excluding others. Ellen had grown into a beautiful woman, yet she spent more time with him than any other man. For weeks now Ellen had been trying to tell him that there was something missing from her life, but he had refused to listen.

Was she wishing for a husband and babies of her own? Her own family? He'd heard the longing in Ellen's voice when she'd asked about Juliet.

Shame and guilt overtook him. Was he holding Ellen back? Was she worried about him being alone and ignoring her own happiness? Was he always an obligation to people?

"And now you only date those awful women." Ellen interrupted his thoughts.

"I date perfectly respectable women."

"Who you meet at places like Workaholics United."

Sam remained silent, refusing to respond to this frequent battle cry. Ellen was determined to make him see Darlene as a mistake, but in his soul, he knew better. Darlene had pretended to love him because he would have provided her with the lifestyle she wanted. She had never lied to him directly—she was only guilty by omission. It wasn't even as if she were cold and calculating and had deliberately set about making him fall in love with her for his money.

Then he could have been angry and outraged, instead of…what?

Hurt. He wouldn't even admit it to Ellen but he'd been hurt.

A week before their wedding, he'd overheard Darlene talking to one of her bridesmaids at the end of one of her many bridal showers. Darlene had gloried in all the female rituals surrounding their nuptials, been delighted every time she'd opened a wedding present, thrilled as she'd sent out their change of address cards. Her happiness had enveloped the two of them and he'd had no doubts about their marriage. He'd foolishly believed she loved him.

He'd arrived to pick her up after one of her bridal showers to help transport the gifts back to the house they'd live in together after the wedding. Darlene hadn't seen him arrive in the hallway and he'd overheard the words between two friends. At first he'd been secretly thrilled as she'd sung his praises, saying how smart he was, how gentlemanly, what a good life she planned for the two of them to share. He'd deliberately remained hidden so he could hear more. He'd heard all right.

The friend, Janine, had asked how Darlene knew she was in love and that Sam was the right man for her.

Darlene had been quiet for a moment, and then she'd spoken in a soft voice that Sam had to strain to overhear. "I don't love him. I thought I might be able to fall in love with him—I wanted to. Sam is very nice, when he remembers I'm around, but it just didn't happen. There have been so many times I've been talking to him and I realize he's been thinking about his damn computer programs. Maybe if I knew more about his work…but it bores me."

"Then why are you marrying him?"

"He'll make a good husband. Plus, he's in love with me. And with the way he looks, I don't think too many women will be coming after him, so I won't have to worry about that. Money's something else I'll never have to worry about. Besides, I'm not getting any younger."

Sam had stood in the darkened hallway a long time before he turned around and went back to the front door, opened it noisily and walked up the stairs to meet Darlene and her friend. He'd taken his fiancée home but hadn't spent the night as he'd planned. Her words had haunted his dreams all night long and by morning he knew he wasn't going to marry her. To his shame, he'd considered marrying her, but his pride wouldn't let him.

He also knew how much it would hurt trying to make her love him but never having it happen. No matter what he'd tried with his parents—and he had tried, over and over again—they had never loved him. He knew that Darlene hadn't meant to hurt him, but she had. She'd betrayed him at the most fundamental level, and he intended never to let himself be hurt like that again. Never.

After he'd ended his engagement, he'd only dated self-absorbed women with whom he could never fall in love.

"I bet you don't even remember the name of the girl you brought to Martin's wedding."

"Stephanie Warren."

"What did she look like?"

"She's a very attractive brunette."

Ellen snorted in a very unladylike manner over the phone, he thought. "She was a redhead. Tall or short?"

"Medium."

"She was over five-ten. She could have been a goddamn supermodel and she made no impression on you."

Ellen was right. He didn't remember a damn thing about the woman. "I was more interested in her mind than her body."

"What is her favorite hobby?"

When you were out on a limb, you might as well jump, he decided. "Rock climbing," he guessed.

"Hah. She knits."

"Stephanie does not knit."

"Yes, she does. We discussed our favorite yarn shops in Portland."

"You don't knit!"

"I hate to break it to you, cousin, but I don't read spreadsheets for fun in the evenings. I've been known to curl up in front of the TV with a skein of wool and a pair of knitting needles." Then, before he could think of anything further to say, Ellen had hung up on him.

He turned his thoughts back to Diva. He had invented her; she was supposed to follow his commands. He spoke slowly and clearly in case she was having difficulty comprehending his voice patterns. "I do not have any appointments on Wednesday at 10:00 a.m. Schedule the meeting with Dexter."

"I repeat, you have a Priority One meeting. Please choose another time slot." If he didn't know his invention couldn't express irritation, he would have said she was annoyed with him.

"Who do I have a meeting with?" He was actually arguing with his computer. He couldn't believe it.

"Dr. Morgan."

"You're wrong. My doctor's name is Scanlon. Dr. Michael Scanlon." He was going to have to recheck the program to see where this error was coming from. The idea of Diva going on sale and making imaginary appointments for clients horrified him.

"The appointment is for Juliet."

The annoyance he'd been feeling disappeared as he gripped the edge of his desk hard. "What's wrong with her?"

"That information is not available to me, but I believe it is a checkup. That indicates preventive care not a response to a specific problem."

His pulse steadied. "Who inputted the information?"

Diva paused for a couple of seconds and then stated, "The information was inputted last night."

One part of him was pleased at her response; she'd given him information that hadn't been a direct response to his question but that had enabled him to learn the answer—it must have been Anne. Diva was smart. He closed the program and went to find the source of all this bedevilment.

Anne was in the reception area standing next to Walter. Sam recognized the look of admiration on the man's face; it was usually reserved for his computer, but this time it was directed at Anne. "Shouldn't you be with the baby?" Sam hadn't meant to sound surly, but Walter had broken out in a sweat as he gazed worshipfully at Anne.

She looked at Sam with surprise and then smiled a warm, pleased smile that he felt through his entire body. "Juliet is sleeping soundly and I have her baby monitor with me. I'll hear her the second she wakes up. You shouldn't worry so much."

"Worrying is Sam's hobby," Walter told her. The man

blinked, seeming to shake himself out of the spell he'd been in. "No matter what time I come in the morning, he's almost always here first, working on a problem he thought of during the night. Sometimes I think Sam dreams computers."

When Anne studied him with sad curiosity, Sam kept his mouth shut, not daring to admit that, indeed, he did dream of computers—sometimes. Not always. Recently a woman with long blond hair had featured prominently in his dreams.

Walter sat up straighter, as if trying to look taller for Anne's appreciation. "You really think that if we put a little bit of parsley in Marcia's baby food, she'll eat?"

"Yes, the parsley cuts the acidity in the fruits found in most baby food. Marcia will like it much better. I'll also write out a few recipes that I've found work really well for finicky babies. And reassure your wife it's not because she didn't breast-feed the child. Lots of babies are problem eaters. The secret is to figure out what's in the food they don't like and then feed them everything else."

Sam stood by awkwardly, wondering how old Walter's daughter was and remembering that he had thought Walter had a son. She was their first child, and Walter often showed up at work looking exhausted. Before Juliet, he'd assumed that Walter had been up late working on one of E²'s projects. Now he realized that Marcia had been the cause of Walter's haggard appearance. "Why don't you take the day off, Walter?"

The man twitched as he looked at Sam with worry. "What? Oh, no. I'm sorry. I didn't mean to distract anyone from the Diva project. I'll get right back on it."

"For heaven's sake, Walter, I'm not angry. I've only recently learned how much time babies consume. Or what they can offer."

"Marcia is the best thing that ever happened to me. Other than my wife, of course."

"Of course. Take the day off and enjoy your little girl and your wife."

"I have a lot of work piled up. With the baby I haven't always been able to concentrate as well as I should. I don't know if—"

"I'm the boss. Take the day off."

Walter grinned and then began to move quickly, shutting off his computer, grabbing his briefcase, and then he slipped out of the office without looking back.

"I must have been disturbing you. I'm sorry." Anne picked up the baby monitor.

He wanted her to stay. Today she wore tailored black pants and a red silk blouse and he found himself wishing he could get a glimpse of her bra. In his fantasies, it was black lace. He stopped those errant thoughts. He liked having her around because her energy and warmth made his office seem different. Just like his home was different with her living in it. "No, it's okay. Surely I'm not such an ogre."

She shook her head. "Your employees adore you. All I've heard is how in awe they are and how much they respect you. They consider you a kind man."

"Hardly. I barely know anything about the people who work here."

"I guess Ellen keeps up with that."

"Yes."

Anne picked up a paperweight from his desk and examined it. "Everyone knows that. Even Ellen said you were a genius and needed to have your work environment made friendly for you."

"So our company arranges itself around my needs?"

"Well, yes. Because you are the one who comes up with the ideas."

Even though that is exactly how he always thought of himself and was relieved to learn that the others enjoyed working at E², somehow he wished he knew more about the people who worked with him. That his co-workers knew him—how he felt, what he liked—instead of thinking of him as an aloof genius. Considering him an oddity. Someone different, always on the outside.

That is how everyone saw him—even Darlene. Perhaps that explained why she didn't love him. She'd wanted to, she said. But it hadn't happened. After the breakup, he'd given her the house they had planned to live in after their wedding. After all, she'd loved the house and spent hours and hours decorating and refinishing, unafraid to saw and hammer. Too late, he'd learned her passion was for the house and not for him.

He pulled himself back from his regrets. He hadn't thought this much about Darlene in months. "Ellen? When did you speak to Ellen?"

"Last night. I wanted to know if it was okay if I held a neighborhood watch program in the lobby area of your business and she's the one who's in charge of things like that."

"A neighborhood watch?"

"Yes. Mrs. Spivak had her car broken into two nights ago, the same night we had our break-in. It seems obvious it was the same people. I thought organizing a neighborhood watch would ease everyone's mind. And we might catch the thieves."

"Who is Mrs. Spivak?"

"She's two houses over on the left. The house with the red door."

He recalled a very blond woman in her early forties.

"Her husband travels a lot—he's an airline pilot—so she gets nervous."

"A neighborhood watch is a good idea."

Sam wasn't so sure about her good ideas by the time Friday evening arrived and he found himself brooding in the kitchen as Anne finished getting dressed for her famous date with Simon. Ellen remained in Seattle phoning him daily with updates. But now she spent as much time talking to Anne as she did to him. And the pair of them giggled worse than a pair of schoolgirls. He had no idea that Ellen could be like that.

Last night, he'd knocked on Anne's bedroom door to tell her that three little girls dressed in red uniforms were on the front porch wanting to know if Anne could possibly attend the next Cardinal Girl meeting to discuss babysitting tips. He'd caught a glimpse of his former spare room as she went to the front door to invite the girls in for homemade cookies and milk. She'd arrived with two suitcases, so he couldn't quite figure out how it was possible, but the room had become Anne's room in every sense of the term. A homemade quilt in muted yellows and blues covered the four-poster bed, lace curtains hung from the windows and pieces of Anne were scattered around the room. Fresh flowers on the dresser and on the table next to her bed. A piece of yellow silk was draped over the lampshade. He longed to step inside and study the photos placed along the bureau, but he didn't. Instead he'd retreated to his office, but all he'd been able to imagine was Simon in bed with Anne.

He frowned at his watch. Simon was picking her up at seven-thirty and taking her to dinner at Street and Co., one of Portland's best restaurants. He was furious. What was Simon imagining? Even more important, what was Anne imagining? Surely she wasn't really attracted to Simon Kensington. Sure he was handsome and rich and single and sociable and charming...and just about perfect. What had he been thinking when he'd introduced them? He should have kept Anne out of the sight of any of his playboy friends. The next thing he knew he'd be booking dates for her.

Not that any of this mattered, whatsoever. He might find Anne very pretty, but he wasn't interested in her. The fact that he'd dreamed about her didn't mean anything.

The fact that he knew what her skin would feel like, that he knew her taste—sweet and intoxicating. That he knew what she would feel like in his arms.

He heard Anne's footsteps coming down the hallway toward the back of the house. "I'm in here," he called and Anne peered through the door at him sitting by the kitchen table.

"Why are you sitting here in the dark?"

"I was thinking."

She flicked on the light switch. "I thought you always did that in front of your computer."

"Everyone seems to think my computer is an extension of me."

"Diva certainly is. She talks like you. I like her." She looked at him and smiled a secretive smile. "Juliet is tucked in bed and looks like she'll sleep for a couple of hours before she wants to get up and play."

"She's not much for sleeping through the night."

"No, but she does love her naps. Are you waiting to say hello to Simon?"

He stood and paced across the kitchen floor. "Simon is a good guy," he said reluctantly as a curious sickness clawed at his gut. Anne was dressed in a simple, ivory-colored, short sheath dress revealing lots of leg and bare arms. "Won't you be cold?"

"I brought a jacket." She held up a raspberry linen jacket that matched her shoes and earrings and the lipstick he wanted to kiss off her lips until all thoughts of Simon fled her mind. "We're going for an early dinner and then to a jazz club. It's been so long since I've been out to hear live music. Even the year I lived in Manhattan with the Lindstroms I got so busy I just never took advantage. Simon seems very cultured. He told me he had season tickets to the symphony. And he coaches a Little League baseball team. Isn't that sweet?"

"A perfect husband, you mean."

She stepped closer to him, hands on hips. "I don't know what is wrong with you, but there is no reason to keep making fun of my desire to get married. I love children and want kids of my own, so of course I want a husband. There is nothing silly or mercenary about my desire."

He also wasn't sure why he needed to ridicule her desires and dreams. A conventional lifestyle might not be for him, but that didn't mean he thought poorly of it. Or of women—and men—who wanted to get married. A small part of him was forced to wonder if he was jealous of her confidence that she would find the perfect mate for herself. And why wouldn't she? After all, she was a beautiful and intelligent woman—even if she did talk too much. The funny thing was, he rather liked the sound of her voice in his apartment. He wondered what it would be like after she was gone. He'd never noticed the silence before.

He was about to apologize when, eyes flashing, her cheeks flushed from anger, she stepped forward, standing toe to toe with him, and poked her finger into his chest. "You are an infuriating man. Just because you don't like Simon, there's no need to make fun of him. Or what I want."

He caught her hand and held it, wrapping his fingers around her slender wrist, feeling the pulse beating quickly. "I like Simon." Unable to help himself, he stroked his finger along the soft skin on the inside of her wrist in a slow motion. Her blue eyes darkened and her mouth fell open as she seemed to search for breath.

His gaze fell to her full, bee-stung lips painted that delicious raspberry, and he felt the blood in his body begin to pound in unison with her pulse.

"Sam..." She tried to tug her hand back but he wouldn't, couldn't, let her go. He couldn't let her go out for an evening with Simon Kensington unless he knew she'd be thinking about him.

As if he held a rope he'd lassoed her with, he tugged the

hand he held in his, fitting their bodies together, chest to chest, hip to hip, her legs pressed tight against his. He held her captured in his gaze and she bit down on her bottom lip. He let out a muffled sound of frustration. She jumped at the noise, but this time he wrapped both arms around her, keeping her to him.

"Sam..."

He leaned his face closer so that their lips were only a breath apart. "I like the way you say my name, all husky and low in your throat." He brushed a featherlight sweep of his lips across hers and saw her pupils dilate, but still she did nothing.

"Nothing to say? I've never known you to be so quiet. You're supposed to be protesting that you don't get involved with clients." He brushed his lips over hers again, a little harder and longer and this time he had to use his willpower to pull back. He wanted her to tell him what she was thinking. "Or you could say, 'Kiss me, Sam. I want you to kiss me...'" He breathed against her mouth.

He didn't wait for an answer, crushing her lips to his, crushing her to him. He had to have every inch of her, every breath. Every sound she could make had to be about him.

He ran his hands along her back, around the curve of her hip and down her buttocks and then back along the length of her, unable to touch enough. The damn dress was in the way and when his hands reached the hem he inched it back up, luxuriating in the expanse of smooth thigh. He felt her tremble in his arms. He held her to him and couldn't resist pressing his erection against her womanly curves. Anne cried out against his mouth and he swallowed the sound.

Still he couldn't stop. She'd opened her mouth to him and he took every opportunity to discover her, reveling in her gasps, in the fact that she had clenched a hand in his hair and was devouring him as eagerly as he was her.

When he slid a hand between their straining bodies and cupped her intimately, she tore her lips away from his, sucking in a great mouthful of air. "No, Sam. You have to stop…oh…"

He slid a finger under the elastic of her panties and stroked her flesh, kissing her again. He kissed her gently this time to show her how much she meant to him, using his mouth and his touch to relay the message. Anne kissed him back. That was all the encouragement he needed. He picked her up and placed her on the kitchen table, her ivory linen dress riding up around her waist.

"What?" she asked, looking at him with passion-drugged eyes, raising her arms to pull him back to her.

He kissed her quickly, running his fingers along her upper thighs, under her dress. "I want to… Let me…"

He replaced his fingers with his mouth and heard Anne gasp as his tongue traced the path where his fingers had been.

"Sam, this is decadent. I'm on the kitchen table. We can't… What are you…? Juliet is asleep… Oh, that feels so good."

Sam didn't need to hear another word, in fact, he couldn't. He needed to touch her, to please her. Wrapping his arms around her hips he angled her toward him, Anne's hands grasped the sides of the kitchen table as he set out to obliterate her every thought of Simon Kensington.

He kissed her intimately, loving the sounds she made, the trembling of her legs. Encouraged by her moans, he continued to stroke and fondle her sweet center, paying particular attention to that nubbin of female flesh. He was lost in a world of feeling and passion; all he wanted to do was taste and touch her until he felt her body tighten…and then she called out his name as she reached the peak.

She collapsed against him and he held her in his arms as

she trembled. He wasn't feeling all that steady himself, fully realizing what he had just done to her. He had never come on like a Neanderthal to a woman before. But he'd never been as jealous before.

He stroked the blond curls tied up loosely at the back of her neck. Finally she went still. Then suddenly she stiffened and pushed away from him. When she stood, for a second, he thought her legs weren't going to hold her, but she pulled herself upright and faced him.

Her face was flushed, the lipstick smeared off her lips and her long blond hair falling around her shoulders. Her breath came in great gasps as she rearranged her dress around her body and then looked at him, her face pale. "How dare you," she got out on a gasp. "That…that was outrageous. Consider this my resignation. I'll stay until the morning when you can call an agency and arrange for another nanny." On the last word, her voice grew unsteady, and she raced out of the kitchen.

"No, Anne. I don't want you to go," he called after her, realizing he had made a terrible mistake.

But Anne wasn't listening to him. She was already gone.

7

"WHAT? Oh, no, no after dinner liqueurs. Thank you, but I'd love some coffee," Anne said absently to Simon. *That man.* That infuriating, insufferable man. Anne couldn't remember a word of what Simon had said to her all night long. All she'd been able to think about, in every Technicolor detail, was every second of her liaison with Sam in the kitchen.

The restaurant was filled with people having a good time surrounded by its comfortable decor of brick walls, blackboard menus and copper pots hanging from the ceiling. Rich aromas filled the air as thickly as the animated conversations.

Simon must have thought of her as an old-fashioned girl—she'd felt the color rise on her cheeks several times during dinner. It had happened each and every time she recalled the wanton image she'd presented on the kitchen table, with her dress pooled around her waist and Sam... Well, she knew where he'd been!

He'd been determined to make his point and he'd made it. How weak she had been. After their unexpected kiss last Saturday, she'd determined to keep her distance, emotionally and physically. And what had happened? Less than a week later, she was letting him make love to her.

No, he'd only been branding her as his territory. The unmitigated arrogance of the man—to think that all he had to do was touch her and all of her defenses would crumble. Of course, they had.

As often as she blushed remembering what Sam had

done to her came the question why. Had he really been overcome with jealousy because of her date with Simon? Did that mean he might care for her?

No, that was a ridiculous idea. Sam had merely felt possessive toward her. He was probably used to women throwing themselves at him.

But wait until she got back home tonight and…and what? What exactly was she going to do with Sam Evans?

And why was she so attracted to him?

He wasn't at all the kind of man she usually dated. She preferred someone with more polish and sophistication and…a man exactly like Simon Kensington to whom she hadn't paid any real attention all evening.

Sam was all rough edges that could cut you if you got too close, but made a woman want to smooth them. Plus, there was a sadness in his eyes that drew her.

"I'm sorry, Simon, I'm afraid I wasn't listening. It's this headache…"

He looked at her with concern. "It's been bothering you all evening. I can tell. If I was a man of a lesser ego I would have been worried that I was boring you, but luckily I know myself better." His lips twitched. "Relax. I may be a computer geek but I don't have a Bill Gates ego. You weren't your usual self."

That was for sure. All she'd been doing was thinking about sex. Sam Evans had kissed her and made love to her…and she wanted him to do it all over again. It had only been pride and a strong sense of self-preservation that had made her walk out of that kitchen rather than drag him into her bedroom, tear off his clothes and do to him everything he'd done to her. And then they could have done it all over again.

She didn't understand her feelings. Sam Evans was attractive and had sex appeal just oozing off him, but she'd dated gorgeous men before and hadn't turned into a sex maniac. How could he turn her on with just one sweep of his eyes or a recitation of a complex mathematical formula? If she'd ever had a math teacher like him in high school she might be working for NASA today.

Truth be told, when Sam Evans kissed her all logical thoughts flew out of her head and all she could do was feel. But having these feelings for a man who only wanted an affair, nothing permanent, was not part of her plan.

She'd probed Ellen for Sam's background but the little that Ellen had revealed was that Sam had had a bad experience with a woman a couple of years ago. They'd been engaged but it hadn't worked out. Well, Sam was much more in love with his work than he ever could be with any woman. He might find her attractive and desirable but she was also the woman sleeping under the same roof as him. She was awfully convenient, especially for a man who didn't value love and relationships.

That was it. Sam knew her stay was only temporary and he found that attractive.

Her latest conclusions—she'd developed several theories over the course of the evening—depressed her. Because? Because she could see all the good in him. How he played with Juliet and made sure everything in the house was baby proof. At first, he'd balked at the time he was supposed to spend playing dad, but he'd done it. He was reliable and dependable. And the sexiest man she'd ever laid eyes on.

If Sam had taken her out tonight and been looking at her the way Simon was, like she was a triple-layer fudge cake with caramel toping and extra whipped cream, she'd be agreeing to go back to his place instead of faking a headache.

"I'm sorry, Simon." She reached across the table and squeezed his hand. "I'm afraid I haven't been the best dinner companion."

"I'm sorry, too. I was looking forward to our evening together and have enjoyed it." He let go of her hand and waved toward the girl selling roses, buying one for Anne. As he paid the young woman, he looked at her with recognition. "Lucy Sinclair?"

She smiled, her elfin face becoming very pretty. "Simon Kensington. I recognized you but didn't want to intrude on your date."

"Not at all. But what are you doing selling flowers? Did something happen to your job?"

"I'm doing a favor for one of my students. She's working two jobs to pay for college, but she's got a bad cold and is trying to study for exams this weekend. I told her I would take over the flower selling gig for the weekend if she'd rest and study."

"You always had a good heart."

"I wouldn't do it for all of my students but she's very talented and needs the money." Lucy looked around the restaurant. "I should move on, but it was good to see you again. I haven't seen you since Darlene and Sam's engagement party."

"Er, yes. Lucy, I'd like you to meet Anne Logan. She works for Sam as his nanny."

"You mean Sam found someone else to marry him?" She slapped her hand over her mouth. "I'm sorry, I didn't mean it like that. It's just I could never understand what Darlene was..." She shook her head.

Anne needed to know more about Lucy Sinclair's bizarre reaction to Sam. "Sam's not married. He has the temporary care of a baby and I'm helping him."

"Oh, I see," Lucy said, not seeing at all. "Lucky girl, you captured Simon's attention."

"Yes." Anne wondered why she wasn't annoyed that Lucy was flirting with Simon. "I take it you were put off by Sam?"

She nodded. "I think he frightened me a little."

"But why?"

"Why? Because of his size and how he's always scowling at you like he's waiting for you to say something wrong."

Wisely Anne kept her mouth shut and just tried to digest the staggering words as Lucy said good-night. Other women didn't find Sam Evans sexy or desirable? What was wrong with the women in this town?

The man was pure one hundred percent male. She'd spent the entire evening on a date thinking about his eyes, his strong chin, not to mention his shoulders. Her mouth watered thinking about him. Plus, he was reliable. Solid and strong like a man should be.

She frowned as she realized that Susan at the office had said something about having to get used to Sam. Mrs. Spivak, the woman she'd organized the neighborhood watch with, had said the same thing.

She tested out the idea and realized no woman had flirted with him in the week she'd been with him. She'd assumed he'd not wanted the attention, had discouraged it, but what if the women of Portland were just plain blind?

Simon presented the rose to Anne with a flourish and a smile of regret. "I was going to spend a considerable amount of energy convincing you to come back to my house. It has a fabulous view of Casco Bay."

"I am sorry," she answered with real regret, their fingers meeting when she accepted the flower. She wished her pulse could have leaped when she touched Simon as it did when she touched Sam. She inhaled the fragrance of the flower and told herself the perfect kind of man was in front of her and she should give him a chance. "Maybe we could do this again?"

"I'd love to. How long are you staying?"

"I don't really know. It all depends on how long Sam will have the baby. Juliet is such a delight."

"You could have knocked me over with a feather when I saw Sam Evans holding a baby."

Her skin prickled at Simon's criticism of Sam. "He's very good with her."

"Don't get me wrong, I'm not trying to run Sam down. It just wasn't the picture I associated with him. And I should have, since he was engaged to Darlene Muesler and she was clearly the kind of woman who wanted children. But still, to see Sam holding a baby..." He shrugged. "It was just plain weird."

"Darlene wanted children?"

"Lots."

"But it didn't work out between them." She took a sip of her coffee so that she wouldn't leap across the table and grab Simon by the tie to extract every last bit of information he knew.

"No. They canceled the wedding only a week before the event. Everyone was surprised and not surprised, if you know what I mean. I never really thought they fit together, but Sam was clearly in love with her."

Anne felt such guilty pleasure learning about Sam that she couldn't help herself from asking more. "What about her? Was Darlene crazy in love with him?" How could she not have been?

Simon frowned as he considered her question. "Sure. Yeah, I guess she was. She was certainly happy to be marrying him. Anyway, a week before the wedding, they called it off. Darlene must have realized..."

"That she'd never be first. His work would always be more important." She said the words to herself and then realized that Simon was studying her.

He smiled. "Here I am telling stories about my friend when I'm not really sure of all the details. All I know is Sam really loved her and was very hurt by the end of their engagement. But all he would say was that it was for the best. He let her keep the house."

"What?"

"They'd bought a house on the Eastern Promenade. A

lot of young families and college kids live there. Darlene moved in a month before the wedding and was doing the painting and the decorating—all that kind of stuff. After they broke up, I know he signed the house over to her. Paid for it and gave it to her. Said she deserved it for putting up with him."

Anne digested the words. Was he still heartbroken over this wonderful Darlene? Or had he ended their engagement? Giving her the house sounded like guilt...

She was pondering the situation, what Lucy had said, what Simon had told her, as they left the restaurant and Simon drove her home. He stopped the car and she looked at the Victorian house in surprise. "We're here," she said inanely.

"I'll walk you to the door."

"I was lost in thought. You've been such a perfect gentleman all evening."

He grinned wickedly as he opened her car door and helped her out. "I'd hoped to be less of one at the end of the evening. You have to promise to give me another chance next week."

"To be less of a gentleman? To attempt to compromise me?" She feigned shock, clutching a hand to her chest.

"Yes." Simon put his hands on her shoulders, his blue eyes growing darker as his gaze fell to her lips. "I'd like to get to know you much better." He continued to look at her for a moment longer and then kissed her. It was a firm, good kiss. As he walked away from her, she touched her lips, feeling the lingering pressure of the kiss but remembering the hunger in Sam's.

Why did she always pick the wrong man? An image of Paul Stone flashed in her mind's eye. At least that mistake had ended quickly. As soon as she'd figured out the truth about what was going on, she'd gotten out.

Had run home to her brother licking her wounds.

While Davis had been sympathetic as she'd poured out

her story about Paul Stone, he'd insisted the best thing she could do for herself was return to what she loved best: taking care of children. His face had positively glowed when he'd relayed the message from Gwen about the job opening with Sam Evans. Davis had looked lighter and happier than during any of the ten days she'd spent in his house.

Davis often had difficulties; Anne had grown accustomed to that. Six years younger than her, she had mothered him throughout their childhood. Davis had never rebelled against it, enjoying the attentions that the women of their household, Betty and she, had showered on him.

Now, he was always full of dreams and possibilities but couldn't dedicate himself to the hard work needed to carry off one of his elaborate schemes. She sighed. If Davis could only take an iota of Sam's drive and work ethic, he could make a success out of his life. Davis was only twenty-four—he could still turn out.

She inserted her key into the front door of the Victorian and let herself in. In the few days Anne had been here, she'd begun to admire the house very much. She could imagine living in a house like this—tree-lined street with a view of the bay, children playing in the yard. Juliet would like growing up in a home like this. But Juliet wouldn't be growing up here, she reminded herself firmly. Gwendolyn Parker would find Juliet's natural mother, convince her to sign the adoption papers and hand Juliet over to the perfect family.

A perfect family that was not her, Sam and Juliet.

She should stop her silly fantasizing. She had no reason to hope that Sam was going to be waiting for her on the top of the steps, eager to resume their earlier activities.

He wasn't. She sighed again. He was probably in his room, sleeping like a baby.

She was wrong again. He was sitting in the rocking chair in her bedroom.

"You. Here." She was rather shocked to find herself speechless.

"Yes." He stood and stepped toward her, looming over her.

She sucked in some air and squared her shoulders. Sam Evans had another think coming if he really believed they were going to pick up from where they'd left off. She suddenly remembered that she had resigned. How had she forgotten that? Well, she'd have to see what he said, but she had no intention of giving over the care of Juliet to some casual rent-a-nanny. Or letting such a woman into the house to flirt with Sam. Even if the woman wouldn't have the good sense to flirt with Sam, if what she had learned this evening really was true. She still couldn't believe that other women didn't find Sam attractive. She had, from the instant she'd clapped eyes on him.

Even more importantly, both Sam and Juliet needed her to take care of them.

Sam scowled at her. "Where is Simon?"

"He's gone home. We had a very lovely evening and agreed to see each other again. Did you imagine I would invite him into my bed on a first date? You seem to have a very low opinion of me, as your actions earlier this evening showed."

He turned a deep red and a muscle by the side of his mouth twitched. "I apologize. It was reprehensible of me." He stiffened his shoulders, looking extremely uncomfortable but determined. "I can assure you that if you reconsider your resignation, nothing of that...sort will ever happen again. I have no excuse, except that you are a very beautiful woman and...I—I found you attractive and I...wanted to kiss you. I never meant anything else. It just sort of..."

"Grew out of control?"

"Yes." He nodded firmly as if glad she understood him, and Anne thought that perhaps she did. She felt a small bubble of hope rise in her. And she felt heat run through her body as she considered that she still wanted him as much as she had earlier in the kitchen. And had for the past week.

"You think I'm beautiful?"

"What? Yes, very beautiful."

"But I'm not the type of woman you usually date. You like them tall and brunette and very sophisticated."

"I've recently acquired a taste for blondes who smell of lavender and vanilla."

"You have?" she asked, suddenly realizing they were in her bedroom and her eyes kept focusing on the bed.

He nodded, moving closer to her, and touched the side of her face. "Still, I behaved abominably." He dropped his hand and stepped back. "Tell me you'll stay and I'll pay you double what my aunt agreed to."

"This has never been about money," she said. "If you continue to insult me I'll make good on my resignation."

"You can't leave. My aunt hired you."

He took a deep breath and let it out slowly. She could see him silently counting to ten and was glad she was driving him as crazy as he made her. Her worst fear had been that Sam had been able to block her out of his mind. "If your aunt knew how you behaved, she wouldn't blame me," she added.

"I have already promised you that my behavior won't be repeated."

"What if I wanted you to repeat it?" She stepped toward him, surprised at her own boldness, but realizing it was necessary for her to make the next move. Sam had already shown he wanted her; now she had to show him the same. "What do you want?" she asked him, her voice low and soft.

He grabbed her by the shoulders to hold her away from him. "That is a foolish question to ask me."

She raised her chin. "Tell me what you want."

"That's dangerous ground."

"Tell me."

"I want you. Every night I've dreamed of you in your lace and satin gowns, in this room. I've imagined everything I could do to you."

"Yes?" Her voice was breathless. "What would you do?"

"Make love to you. Slow and soft. Fast and hard. There isn't an inch of you that I wouldn't kiss."

"Yes... What else?"

He scowled at her but she saw desire in his eyes. She smiled and he scowled more fiercely. "I'd make you scream when you came."

The smile dropped off her face. "Promises, promises. Prove it."

She wrapped her hands around his neck and pulled him to her. Then his strong arms wrapped themselves around her and she was enveloped by heat and the very male scent of him. She lost sense of time and place as all she could do was lose herself in him. She dragged her hands through his hair and kissed him hard.

He broke out of their kiss, his eyes stormy and filled with desire. "I want you."

"Yes."

"If you don't want me, say so now. In a moment, I won't be able to stop myself. I lose control around you."

She laughed. "You're not giving me much chance to say no, when you have your hand on my breast like that." He squeezed gently and then brushed his thumb over her hard nipple. "Oh, you're confusing me."

He nipped her neck. "I want to confuse you as much as you confuse me."

"Making love will do that?"

"Say yes." He nudged her legs apart with one of his own and pulled her high against him. He brought his mouth back to hers and kissed her. "Say yes."

"Yes."

The next thing she knew she was being lifted and laid gently on her bed. Then Sam was on top of her, his big body covering hers firmly. She ran her hands over his broad, firm, strong shoulders. "You feel so good."

His lips traced a path from her ear, down her neck and over her linen dress to where her nipple pressed against the fabric of her dress.

She moved her hands to the front and began to undo the buttons on his shirt. He let her ease the shirt off his shoulders as she sat up and kissed his chest, running her tongue over his solid muscles, scraping her teeth over his nipple. She felt him suck in his breath and then he was pulling her jacket off her shoulders. Once he had it off, he ran his hands very slowly up her bare shoulders raising goose bumps along every inch of the way.

All she could do was feel and wonder, but she had to tell him, "Sam, you're so handsome."

He made a funny sound and then reached for the zipper on the back of her dress and pulled. Clearly he didn't believe her, but she'd show him how she saw him. She felt an inch or two of air against her bare skin, when he cursed.

"It gets stuck sometimes," she managed to say. "You have to play with—" Her words were cut off by his lips. If she'd thought she'd been overwhelmed before, she had no idea. Now it was like a storm. She was swept away by the force of his passion, like a doll caught up in the waves of the Atlantic.

She felt him pull on her dress, but when it wouldn't give, his hands swept the dress over her hips and breasts and her head, tangling in her arms.

She didn't care. All she could do was feel the hard solid length of him over her and gasp when his mouth found her bare breast and took it into his mouth. "Sam," she cried, not knowing what she wanted. He used his hands to fondle her breasts as his tongue and teeth worked on her

nipples. She arched against him, offering more of herself
to his ministrations.

She realized her hands were bound behind her back by
her dress. "My dress," she gasped, but Sam didn't hear
her. She struggled to free her arms but only succeeded in
wrapping the dress more firmly around her elbows. Her
actions, however, excited Sam as he growled and parted
her legs, stroking her nest of curls and then easing a finger
into her.

"You're ready for me," he said.

"Sam, I want my arms," but her words died off as he
lowered his head to her breasts again and used his hand
between her legs to arouse her further.

"Now," she demanded, giving up on trying to free her
arms. She didn't care that Sam was in charge of their lovemaking; she only knew she would surely die if he didn't
enter her soon. "I want you now."

He continued to run his hands and mouth over her body
until she thought she would lose all control if he didn't answer the ache within her body.

"Sam, now. I must insist."

He raised his head over hers and smiled wickedly. "Insist? How do you plan to insist in this position? I think I
have you under my complete control."

"You'd like that, wouldn't you?" The sentence ended on
a gasp as he inserted a finger inside her again and caressed. "Oh…that's unfair tactics."

"I never said I played fair." He kissed her mouth and
continued to caress her as she raised her hips in rhythm to
his sweet torture. She kissed him back, using her tongue to
show him what she wanted. Finally she felt his hand leave
and then the hard tip of his penis pressing against her soft
folds.

He entered her in a smooth stroke and she gasped in satisfaction as he filled her. He held her by her hips, angling
her so that he could fill her even more, and then began to

move. With him holding her and her hands behind her back, he really was in full control, but she wasn't afraid. Instead she felt safe enough to let herself go, to experience everything, his strength and passions. The blood pounded through her body as the excitement built. She called out his name over and over again as he pleased and tormented her.

Finally he increased the speed of his thrusts and she felt herself on the brink as he reached between their two bodies to stroke her with his hand. Anne screamed as she went over the edge.

8

ANNE STRETCHED LUXURIANTLY, feeling as if she had planned the perfect garden party. She looked outside her window to see the bright, cloudless sky and learned the First Lady had accepted her invitation. Then her hand brushed against the solid flesh of a male chest. Sam. She was in bed with Sam after a night of lovemaking that brought a blush flooding into her cheeks.

Never before in her life had she been so sexually aggressive or hungry, but with Sam her every inhibition had been torn away and she'd delighted in his body. As much as he'd delighted in hers.

She opened her eyes slightly and saw that Sam was still asleep. Unable to resist, she brushed her fingertips over the dark hair on his chest. He was so solid and strong; she couldn't get enough of touching him.

Despite her claim that she didn't go to bed on the first date, she had done exactly that. Moreover, she and Sam hadn't even gone on a date and she'd only known him for a few days—and here she was naked in bed with him.

But that was the answer wasn't it? She and Sam had had sex. They'd been overwhelmed by all the hormones electrifying the air around them and given in. There was nothing confusing about it. And now that they had...? Well, that would be it. Besides she was only going to be in Sam Evans's house—and, therefore, his life—for a few weeks. Then she would leave for another job.

If she was smart she wouldn't repeat the actions of the previous night. Except, thinking back, she had been pretty helpless to do anything but experience what Sam did to her, she reflected ruefully. Even after Sam had finally stripped her naked, he had continued to make love to her. She'd been overwhelmed by the sensations, overwhelmed by Sam and how gentle and loving he could be, and she had let herself experience the pleasure of it. She never had a chance to explore his beautiful body.

Hmm. Maybe they needed to do it again so she could fully appreciate every delicious inch of him.

She shifted against him.

"Are you all right?" His deep voice was soft as he took the hand that was stroking his chest, raised it to his lips and kissed her fingers.

She melted inside and moved closer to him, raising her head over his. "Last night, there were some things I didn't get to—"

The phone rang, interrupting her amorous suggestion. Sam bolted out of her bed, leaving her behind without a word. Damn and double damn. What had she been thinking? Imagining that Sam would be pleased—that he wouldn't seize the first opportunity to run away from her? Anne got out of her bed, went to the dresser, pulled out a nightgown, put it on and threw a robe over it. Then she followed Sam into his room. Never let it be said that Anne Logan took the coward's way out even after she'd been an idiot. No matter how appealing she found Sam Evans she should have resisted. Found the willpower and resisted the lure of his charms.

He sat on the end of his bed, still naked, the cordless phone nestled against his shoulder as he made notes on a yellow legal pad. "What kind of signs?" He listened and wrote. Anne watched the play of muscles across his back, drawn to him even now that he had forgotten her. "Carmichael, who's he again?" His voice was sharp and she realized he was speaking with Ellen. "The vice president of new acquisitions. He told you they've been approached by another company that claims to have the same technology? Who? How could they? We haven't heard a word."

Sam wrinkled his brow and wrote furiously on the pad as he listened to Ellen's response. "Can't you get him to tell you the name of our competitor? I don't know how...use your feminine wiles or something." He listened to her response and then laughed. "Using your feminine wiles is how you found out we do have competition. Don't bite my head off, Ellen, I'm sure you've done everything you should do. You've done a great job."

He stood up, carrying the portable phone across the room to his computer, and flipped the On switch. For the first time he noticed Anne and he waved her into the room as he continued listening to Ellen, while she continued listening to the one-sided conversation. What did this mean? That someone—a rival company—was trying to sell the Diva technology to ComputExtra? She thought that no information had been stolen during the break-in on Saturday night. Indeed, she'd been hoping it was only a simple burglary—not an act of corporate spying.

"Yes, I think it may be directly connected to the break-in on Saturday night," Sam said, echoing her thoughts. "No, don't fly back yet. Stay a few extra days and see if you can get Carmichael or whoever to spill his guts.

"Ellen, be careful. Of course, I'll be careful, too. I worry about you." He hung up and shook his head as he stared at his computer screen.

Anne stood barefoot in his room, feeling awkward and out of place. Surely Ellen and Sam were mistaken—no one was trying to steal their hard work. She walked over to him and put her hand on his shoulder, wanting the solid reassurance of his body as she worried about their situation—both personal and professional. "What are you looking at?"

"An internet secret room."

"A secret room?"

"Sort of like in the movies when there's a secret room in the spooky mansion on top of the hill. It's a place where hackers and other techno nerds leave messages. Or brag about what they've accomplished."

"I don't understand."

"A lot of these guys get their thrills by breaking into places they shouldn't—like police records. Because their activity is illegal they can't tell anyone for fear of being arrested. But they do post notices here sometimes saying what they've accomplished."

"And you think someone might have posted a notice about Diva?"

"It was worth a look, but no, no one has. I was hoping…"

"That it was just some kid fooling around. Nothing serious."

"Exactly. If there was something here, then it would mostly be bragging. Or the kid wanting a job working with me."

"But since it's not?"

"You understood what Ellen was telling me? She's had this funny feeling about the deal ever since she'd arrived in Seattle, but she couldn't get any real information out of them. But this Carmichael guy took her out for dinner, and she kept pumping him, until he finally revealed that they had gotten an offer just after she arrived, offering to sell them the same program for far less than we're asking."

"When did this happen?"

"Carmichael remained vague on the details but it sounds like they got the offer on Monday morning."

"After Saturday night's break-in?" Her voice was breathy, and Sam linked his fingers through hers as if to provide reassurance.

"Yes. Saturday was rather a momentous day. First you arrived and took over control of my life and then someone broke into my company."

She shifted her weight from one foot to the other as she considered what he was telling her. "Weird coincidence, right?" As her nerve ends tingled, she waited for him to make the connection. When he continued to stare at the computer screen, she tried again. "But I thought whoever broke into your computer files wasn't able to get the information. That he—or she—wasn't able to get into the Diva files. You stopped them before they could."

"Yes. I stopped them." Sam spun around in his chair, his face worried. When he saw her expression he straightened out his frown, stood and cupped her face between his palms. "Don't worry so much about this."

She couldn't help herself; she was frightened. "But someone is trying to steal your idea. They planned the break-in. Even though they didn't get your files, they've still made an offer to sell it to ComputExtra. That means they're coming back."

Gently he pulled her body against his and she let herself lean into his strength. A woman could learn to depend on a man like him. "Don't worry," he repeated against her hair.

Again, she waited for him to say more. When he didn't, she had to point out the obvious conclusion. "Somehow they still expect to get Diva from you. As if they had an in."

"Yes, I was just thinking that. Did Simon ask a lot of questions about my work while you were out together on your date?"

"No. Surely you don't suspect Simon?"

"It could be anyone. Simon and I have the two most successful software businesses in this neck of the woods, but there are several newer companies that could use the prestige of a project like Diva." He shrugged. "I don't really think it's Simon, but I have to consider everyone."

She broke out of his arms and stepped away from him.

"Could you put on some clothes? It's hard to have a serious conversation when you're naked."

He raised a brow but didn't say anything as he walked into his bathroom and returned wearing a navy robe.

"Aren't you suspicious of me? I arrived just as all this funny business began."

Sam shook his head. "I don't believe that of you for a minute. If I did, it would mean you slept with me to gain my trust. No, something else is going on."

She clasped her hands together tightly. "You never thought it could be me?"

"I admit it crossed my mind for a moment since the timing was so connected, but it would mean that you had to know my aunt was planning to drop off a baby on my doorstep, know who I was and then put this plan into action after she hired you. I don't see how you could have. Moreover, you really are a nanny. I checked your references. Making you into a corporate spy, as well, is a little too hard to believe."

"Nanny by day. Super sleuth by night." She laughed but wished she could get rid of the crazy theory that was running through her head.

Sam crossed the room, turned off his computer and then faced her. "About what happened in your room."

He sounded so serious that she forgot all about her crazy ideas as she swallowed and tried to read his expression. "What happened was we had sex."

"Yes. I…I'm not sure what I thought was going to happen when I waited for you. I do know, however, what I wanted to happen. I wanted to make love to you. I haven't been able to think of much else ever since you arrived."

"And now that we have?"

"I think that's up to you. What do you want?"

His dark eyes, filled with concern and something like fear, seemed to reach out to her. She quashed her worries and cautions. For him, she was willing to risk losing. "I want you."

Sam grinned. "How about if we go back to bed?"

"Together?"

"Yes. I rather like this yellow nightgown you put on. You don't know the amount of time I've spent fantasizing about these silk gowns of yours."

She smoothed the silk along her thigh. "I like pretty things."

"So do I." He leaned over and kissed her, taking her breath away. His lips were so gentle and sweet, she found herself blinking away tears. She decided she didn't want to think anymore. She wanted her chance to make love to Sam Evans.

"I'M HOME," Sam shouted from the hallway as he walked up the steps into their apartment.

"Sam is home, Juliet," she told the gurgling little baby who had smiled at the sound of Sam's voice. Anne smiled as well, taking one last look at the kitchen table that she had set for dinner. Sam had called earlier and told her not to cook, that he would take care of dinner. So she and Juliet both bathed and dressed in their best, waiting for Sam. This was even more domestic than she'd ever imagined.

He walked in carrying two large white plastic bags. "Here." He handed her one of them. "I brought us dinner."

She took the package and could smell ginger and chicken. "You're not cooking?"

"You should be happy I'm not cooking. I stopped off at J&B Catering—" Anne raised her eyebrows at the name of the exclusive catering shop in Portland "—and picked up a selection. I wasn't exactly sure what you would like." He smiled at her and her knees weakened. "I guess there are a lot of things I still have to learn about you."

She set down the bag and kissed him on the cheek. "I

think what I like is you." Juliet wiggled in her arms trying to get closer to Sam. The little girl knew what she liked. "Here, Juliet's been missing you all day long. I tried turning the TV on to PBS, but none of the shows were dry enough for her intellectual tastes."

"That's because my little girl is a genius, isn't she?" He lifted her high in the air over his head and Anne didn't make any comment about his calling Juliet his little girl. Men could become attached to babies even more quickly than many women did. He probably wasn't even aware of his feelings for her yet.

As much as she would like to ask him about his feelings for her, it was too soon. She didn't really know what she felt for him, either—only that she had never felt this, whatever this was, before.

"The other package is for you." He pointed to two large boxes each tied with a red ribbon. With trembling fingers she lifted the lid off the first box and found an ivory-colored dress with a designer label. It was much like the dress she had worn last night but more sophisticated and much more expensive. The silk fell like water over her hand. He shrugged when she looked at him questioningly. "I believe I owe you a dress. The one you were wearing last night was pretty well destroyed during our...amorous pursuits."

She wished he would have called their amorous pursuits lovemaking.

"Open the other box."

She did. It contained a negligee in the softest of silks in a pastel-pink with lace trim under the empire waistline, and pink ribbons tied on the shoulders holding up the whole frothy concoction. "It's beautiful. But you've spent too much money—"

"I have lots of that. The dress I owed you. The night-gown, however, I have to admit is perhaps more a gift to myself than for you. I was hoping you might put it on later tonight."

She felt herself blush from head to toe and busied herself with the food containers, opening them and placing them on the kitchen table. "This smells wonderful."

He let her change the subject and, after he put Juliet to bed, they began their dinner.

"It's delicious," Anne told him. "Did you get any further in your investigation as to who is trying to steal Diva?"

"I asked a lot of questions—I have a lot of contacts in the computer field—but no one knows anything. Or not anything they're willing to tell me."

"Are you going to hire a private investigator?"

"No. I'm used to solving my own problems. I'll solve this one as well. Besides I don't really have a case for anyone to investigate. Just a lot of suspicions and one attempted break-in during which nothing was stolen. It could have just been a random burglary."

"You don't believe that."

"No. But I do look at the evidence head-on."

"So now what do you do?"

"I think we wait for the next move by whoever is after Diva. I've made a number of inquiries and learned that one of the small local companies run by Bill Madison is in trouble. He's lost a couple of big contracts in the past few months and he's bad-mouthed E^2. Then again, it could be someone else. If someone is really after Diva, he'll have to try again."

She shivered. "I don't like the sound of that. The last time, the thugs hit you over the head and knocked you unconscious. Maybe I'm being paranoid, but what if they do worse? Or come after Juliet?"

His fierce gaze met hers. "I never thought of you and Juliet in danger. You'd better move to a hotel tonight."

"Don't be ridiculous. I'm not leaving you alone."

"I don't want you or Juliet hurt."

"Then you'll have to come with us." She raised her chin stubbornly. "Or else we're all staying here." She paused. "Let's think logically—I think I was overreacting a moment ago. This is a computer crime… It's unlikely anything violent will happen again. You were knocked unconscious before because you surprised the burglars. If there is a next time, I'm sure they'll wait until everyone is out of the house."

"That's a good idea." He raked a hand through his hair. "Stay for now. But if anything else dangerous happens you have to promise me you will leave with Juliet."

"I promise."

They finished dinner and Sam stood. "I'll clear."

"I'll help."

"I'd rather you checked on Juliet and then changed into that nightgown I gave you. I've been imagining you in it for the past hour—now I'd like to see the reality."

At the look of desire in his eyes, she swallowed. "I…I'll be right back."

In Juliet's room she wondered what exactly she was getting herself into. Sam wasn't looking for any kind of long-term commitment, while that was exactly what she was searching for. Couldn't she just enjoy the moment? Juliet woke and began to cry. Anne held her in her arms and sat down in the rocking chair, soothing the little girl back to sleep, all the while considering what she should do. Sam's gifts were very generous—and another example of him being in complete control of their relationship. Could she even call it a relationship? Not really, but if she bailed out now, she would never know where it could go. All she knew really was that she had feelings and reactions to Sam Evans unlike any she had ever had for any other man. For her own sake, she needed to learn what could happen between them.

When Juliet had fallen asleep, Anne placed her back in

her crib and went to her bedroom to change into the nightgown Sam had bought for her. It fell in soft folds from the
empire waist to the floor. She twirled in front of the mirror
feeling like a princess. The nightdress was luxurious, elegant and very feminine. Sam did know her taste.

Taking a deep breath, she left her room and headed toward the living room where Sam had said he would light
a fire. Drinks in front of a fire was very romantic and she
intended to make the most of the evening, afraid she and
Sam wouldn't have many more in the future. She walked
into the room and stopped dead in her tracks. "Davis."
Her brother turned from facing the fire. When he saw her,
he grinned wickedly. She pulled the robe she had thrown
over the gown more tightly around herself. "I wasn't expecting to see you here!"

"So I see."

"I was just coming in to see if Mr. Evans needed anything before I went to bed. Juliet is sleeping and should
stay that way for several more hours. For a five-month-
old, she's getting better at sleeping through the night. I
had one baby who didn't sleep through the night until he
was fourteen months. Of course, his parents were having
marital difficulties, so he could have sensed the tension in
the house. Babies can tell..." She stopped her rambling.

"Davis dropped by with some more of your things."
Sam put another log on the fire and threw in a match,
lighting it.

Davis leaned against the mantel, enjoying her discom-
fort. "I left the bags down by the front steps."

Sam looked at the brother and sister. "I'll go get them
and put them in your room."

"Thanks." She watched him leave and then took a step
toward her brother. The look on his face made her stop.

"I'm surprised at you, sis. It looks like you and the boss
are getting awfully cosy. After what happened last time, I
thought you would be more careful."

"You're being ridiculous. There is nothing going on between me and Sam." Was she lying to Davis or herself?

"Then why are you dressed like that? And he was lighting a fire. There were two snifters of brandy on the coffee table."

She raised her chin. "I'm more interested in why you're here again, Davis. It's not like you to stop by my place of work on a regular basis."

"Anne, you wound me. You've never actually worked in the same city as me before."

"You never picked up the phone to call me long distance very often, either."

"I've never liked the phone. Here I am for once being the dutiful younger brother, who's only got his sister's best interests in mind, and you're giving me a hard time." He stepped toward her and brushed a lock of hair off her face. "I'm only worried about you, Anne. You can do whatever you like with Sam Evans, but I don't want you to be hurt again."

"I won't be. I don't expect anything from him."

Davis shook his head. "I don't believe you. But it is your life and I certainly don't like it when you interfere in my love life. So I'll stay out of yours. But be careful."

"You'd like Sam if you knew him better."

"Maybe I would. But not tonight. I think you two have better plans. Maybe you'll invite me over some evening for dinner and I'll get to know the brilliant Samuel Evans better."

"Is he really that smart?" Heavens, but she had it bad. She was pathetically eager to talk about Sam.

"Even smarter. When I was in school we studied several of his inventions. He doesn't think like the ordinary computer developer. He can see things none of the rest of us can imagine. And then he can make them work." Davis looked down at his shoes. "I guess you can kind of say I idolized him when I was in college."

"And now?"

"Now I'd like to get to know him better, especially if he's sleeping with my sister."

"You have nothing to worry about in regards to your sister. I would never hurt her," Sam said, walking back into the living room. His face remained impassive, revealing nothing as his gaze swept over her. "I put your bags in your room."

She wished she knew what he was thinking. Most of the time she could read Sam very well. The only time she couldn't was when an element of their relationship entered the equation. "Davis, I think it's time you went home."

Davis kissed Anne on the cheek and, with a last mutinous look at Sam, he left the room. Anne walked him to the top of the steps that lead down to the main floor. "I'll let myself out," he said. "Listen, I'm sorry if I embarrassed you, but…"

"But you worry about me, just like I worry about you. What you suggested about the three of us getting together would be a good idea. He's got this really big project he's working on at the moment, but as soon as he has a little time…"

"I thought he'd finished Diva."

"You know about her? It?" Now, she was beginning to sound like all the men in her life who were more in love with their computers than with people.

"Everyone in the computer business knows. When something this revolutionary happens that's going to affect regular people, people who aren't computer geeks, then I'm impressed. Man, I'd love to work with him someday."

"Aren't you working now?"

"I'm only working on my own stuff—that can always wait."

"But I thought you had a contract with IBM for six months."

"My boss was an idiot. I couldn't deal with him, so I gave it up. You only work with kids, Anne. You don't know what it's like to have an idiot, who got ahead only because he's a yes-man, telling you what to do when you know much better yourself."

Anne sighed. It was always the same story with Davis. "I do have parents to contend with and some of them can be more of a handful and more childlike than my young charges."

Davis squeezed her hand, his eyes wide and pleading. "Would you ask him, Anne? He hires freelancers sometimes and I'd love the chance to see how E² works. Come on, what do you say? It looks like he has a soft spot for you."

Anne gave in, as she always did to her brother. "I'll try. If there's a moment where asking him is appropriate. So don't phone me tomorrow morning wanting to know if you've got the job."

"Tonight could be very appropriate." Davis winked at her.

She punched him in the arm. "You are a terrible younger brother and you have to leave right now." Davis kissed her on the cheek, laughing at her.

"You are almost too easy to tease. Call me in a couple of days and let me know how everything is working out. Love ya, sis."

Anne closed the door behind him and leaned against it for a second, listening to Davis's retreating steps. She wished he would take his life more seriously, but then he wouldn't be Davis—charming, laughing, irresponsible Davis. Then he would be her.

She looked down at herself, at the pink-tipped bare toes peeping out from under the silk on her long pale pink gown. No, she hadn't fooled Davis for a second. She looked exactly like a woman who expected a long night of romance.

But what did Sam Evans really want? She knew that he trusted her with Juliet and was grateful that she had shown up to help him. Not for a second had he thought she had anything to do with the mysterious break-in. But he questioned her motives for wanting to find a husband. Why?

Because of what had happened to him with the former fiancée Darlene Muesler? Anne disliked the woman for no reason other than the fact that she had once been engaged to Sam. Simon had said that she was rather like Darlene, but she doubted it. Had Darlene broken Sam's heart? Or had Sam realized that he would always be more interested in his work, in what next miracle he could invent, and called off the wedding before he could hurt Darlene even further? From what she had learned of Sam Evans, the second possibility seemed much more likely. He was a man who was driven by his mind, not his heart. It would be the loss of Diva and not Darlene that would wound him most deeply.

She had to remember that. She had to remember that the short time they had together was a temporary arrangement. As soon as Gwendolyn Parker found Juliet's mother and got her to sign the adoption papers, Juliet and Anne would be out of Sam's life for good. He would think of them sometimes, she was sure, probably with a great deal of fondness, but he didn't want them to be part of his life.

So why was she walking back into the living room instead of going back to her own bed alone? Why was she begging for heartache?

Because Sam drew her. There was something about him that called to her and it was more than just his sheer physical presence, although that was impossible to ignore. She always believed in conquering the impossible, and if Sam wasn't impossible, then she didn't know what was.

How ridiculous, she mused. Sam wasn't another craft project. Another skill to develop.

Her feet had led her to the living room. Sam was sitting on the couch, his shoulders hunched forward, brooding at the fire. What was he thinking about that hurt him so? she wondered.

"Sam?"

The tension eased from his back as he turned around to face her. "I wasn't sure if you would come back. Your brother doesn't seem all that fond of me."

"On the contrary, he admires you greatly. He considers you one of his heroes. In fact, he wanted me to ask you for a job." She could have bit her tongue as his face darkened at the last of her words.

"I'm learning that many strangers admire me, but few people know me."

He was upset about that and not the part about her asking for a job for Davis. "Ellen knows you and loves you. I know you."

"And?" He raised a dark brow.

"I like you."

"Do you?" He stood and moved until he was only inches from her. "I'm not husband material." His hand curved around her waist.

"I know. It's rather stupid of me to get involved with you."

"Not at all part of your plan."

"No." She raised on her tiptoes and brushed a kiss along the side of his mouth and then down his neck.

"You should be dating Simon."

"Oh, yes, that would be the much smarter thing to do." She wrapped her arms around his shoulders and pressed herself against him and kissed him on the mouth. When she came up for air she murmured, "Simon, in fact, is the perfect man for me."

Sam swept her up into his arms and glowered down at

her. "If you see him again, I'll have to lock you up in my house forever."

"Promises, promises. You keep making them to me every time we're about to make love."

She couldn't see his face very well, the shadows of the hallway hiding its hard lines as he walked down the hall past her bedroom toward his. She wondered if she'd said the wrong thing—again. "I thought you liked my room," she blathered.

"I do." He opened his door with his foot and kissed her hard. "But I want you here, in my room. I want to make love to you here. I want to remember you here."

She wondered if he would remember her after she was gone. But then all rational thought fled and all she could do was feel.

9

"I CAN HARDLY BELIEVE you're the same man," Ellen said to Sam as he removed the old diaper from Juliet, carefully folded it together and handed the soiled object to her. She took it gingerly between two fingers, holding it far away from her body and her expensive suit as she tried to figure out what to do with it.

"Throw it in the trash can over there." He pointed to the white plastic bin in the corner of the nursery.

Ellen did as she was told. Out of the corner of his eye he saw her shaking her head as she pulled a baby wipe out of its container and wiped her hands. "I was only gone ten days," she muttered. He heard her, but preferred to ignore her words. He cleaned Juliet's bottom with several disposable wipes and then powdered her. He was amazed to discover that he loved the smell of baby powder. If anyone combined baby powder, lavender and vanilla as a scent he'd be a goner. Of course, sometimes Anne smelled of them all. Put Anne out of your mind, he told himself for the hundredth time. They were having an affair, so it was natural for him to be infatuated with her, but that was as far as his feelings went. He didn't meet her list of requirements for a husband. Nor did he want to.

He finished fastening the new diaper on Juliet and eased her waving legs back into the feet of her sleeper.

Ellen stood next to him, looking down at the happy baby. "How did you learn how to do that?"

"It's only a matter of simple engineering, nothing very complicated. Most parents learn how to do this very

quickly." He held his hand open in front of Juliet's face
and she grabbed for his middle finger, pulling it toward
herself, gurgling as she did so.

"But you're not a parent." Ellen shook her head. "If I
didn't know better, I'd say you'd been taking care of
babies all your life."

"Thanks to our interfering Aunt Gwen, I am for now."

Ellen ran her hand over Juliet's head. "She's so sweet.
Do you think I could hold her?"

"Of course." When Ellen continued to remain standing
awkwardly by the crib, he scooped Juliet out and placed
her in Ellen's arms. "Cradle your arm a little more like
this," he said, demonstrating, "Juliet likes to look around
at her surroundings. And don't worry about supporting
her head. I found out that at five months old babies can
hold up their head on their own."

"Amazing. You're showing me how to hold a baby."
She smiled at him and Sam couldn't help smiling back,
then they both began to laugh.

"If Aunt Gwen could see us now, she'd be thrilled," he
finally said when he could breath again.

"I won't tell her, if you don't." Ellen frowned. "The
baby arrived last Friday night, the same night I left for Seattle. Do you think Aunt Gwen knew that I would be gone
for over a week?"

"Undoubtedly. Otherwise, I would have foisted this little girl on you and gone back to my computer. Her name is
Juliet."

"Juliet. That's so pretty. Just like this beautiful little
girl." Ellen kissed Juliet on the top of her blond curls, then
sat on the spare bed, settling the baby on her lap. She took
the infant's hands between her own and began to show
her how to play patty-cake. Juliet cried with delight and
drooled all over the skirt of Ellen's very expensive suit. Ellen didn't notice. Instead she looked back up at Sam.
"Don't you want to talk about what happened in Seattle?"

"Of course I do, but just let me settle Juliet down for her nap. She's usually very good in the afternoons."

Reluctantly she handed Juliet over to him. "I'm still having difficulty believing I'm having this conversation with you while you put a baby to sleep. My genius cousin who rarely takes his face away from his computer screen? When I didn't see you at the airport, I expected you to be in our office, working on alterations to Diva II."

Juliet had already closed her eyes and he tucked a blanket around her. "Anne will be back soon, then we can go downstairs and discuss our strategy. You didn't get anything more out of Carmichael?"

"No. After telling me that there was another offer on the table, he shut up. I kept after him but he seemed more interested in dinner and dancing than spilling any more secrets."

"No pillow talk?" He rarely asked Ellen about her romantic life, but now he found he wanted to know.

She blinked in surprise. "No pillow talk. He was fun and I like to dance, but there's no point when he's in Seattle and I'm here."

Sam found the stuffed lamb Juliet liked to sleep with and put it inside her crib where she would find it as soon as she woke, then he turned to face his cousin. "Do you want to stay here forever?"

Ellen got up off the bed. "Of course I do. This is my home." Her eyes narrowed. "What are you talking about? What are you thinking? Do you want to do something different? Do you want to break up our partnership?"

"No, of course not. I've just been wondering recently if I've been holding you back. You told me yourself that you feel something is missing from your life."

Ellen began her nervous pacing again; she paced whenever she was agitated. "I want a husband not an end to the best friendship and best partnership I've ever had! Has that Anne Logan somehow twisted your brain cells? Poisoned you against me? She seemed very nice on the phone, a little meddlesome maybe, but I thought she had a good heart." She stopped in front of him, her face grave, and reached out to touch his shoulders. "Tell me."

"Anne is great."

"What?"

"She's a wonderful person."

Ellen's eyes, so much like his own, searched his face. "Are you involved with her?"

"No. Yes. Maybe."

"That's a perfectly unclear answer—and very unlike you." She let go of him. "You're so unlike the man I left behind a week ago. Either you are or you aren't involved with her."

He sighed. "Yes. I'm involved with her."

"But that's great. Isn't it? Anne Logan is wonderful, you just told me so yourself. And she's helping you with the baby. So I don't understand why you're so worried." Ellen fiddled with the emerald ring on her finger. "It's more than someone being after Diva. Tell me what's worrying you."

"She's an awful lot like Darlene."

"Darlene Muesler." Ellen resumed her pacing of the nursery, gesticulating with her hands. "Queen of all stupid women," she ranted. "The idiot who didn't know a good thing when she held your heart in her hands. Darlene, little Miss Butter Wouldn't Melt In Her Mouth, who was more busy checking out your balance book than your good character. That Darlene?"

He kept his voice even. Ellen was too hard on Darlene. "You always did rush to my defense. It wasn't Darlene's fault if she couldn't love me. I thought she could, she thought she could, but it didn't happen."

"That's because she wasn't the right woman for you. Not because there was anything the matter with you."

He smiled weakly. "It's a good argument, but I'm

thirty-three years old. You and I are the only ones who ever stood up for each other."

"You're forgetting Aunt Gwen."

"No, I'm not. Gwen and Theodore never had any children and they wanted kids. We were the convenient substitutes."

Ellen sucked in her breath. "You're being ridiculous. Aunt Gwen and Uncle Theo loved us very much because of who we were. We weren't any kind of substitutes. The fact that Darlene crushed your spirit has more to do with her being the first girl you fell in love with. You've always spent more time with your formulae than you have people. You can figure out the false lead in a complex mathematical problem but you don't know people."

"That's your job."

"For our company, yes. But you can't let Darlene keep you back from other relationships."

Sam was tired of this repeated argument he'd had with Ellen. He hadn't shared everything that had transpired between himself and Darlene, but Ellen instinctively knew some of it. Moreover, Ellen refused to believe that Darlene was entitled to her feelings. He'd learned to accept the fact that, with his oafish hands and giant body, he scared most women.

He didn't scare Anne Logan.

She wasn't a woman who was easily scared. For some reason, she found him attractive. Perhaps it was because she had first met him while he was holding Juliet and this had softened his image in her eyes. If they had met on the street, or at a party, she would have been as uncomfortable as most women were around him.

What was he going to do about Anne Logan?

"When does Aunt Gwen think she will take the baby away to her new home?"

"She left me a message about Juliet on the baby web page this morning. She's pretty sure she knows that Veronica, the mother, is in San Francisco so she's flying out there today to look for her."

"San Francisco is a pretty big city."

"Yes. But you know Aunt Gwen. She's very resourceful."

"Are you sure she doesn't have the mother staying at her own apartment and is sending you e-mail about the false goose chase she's on?"

"Why would she do that?" He had wondered the same question more than once.

"Because she likes to meddle in our lives. Because she thinks that unless you spend time with a baby you'll never want one of your own. She wants to be Auntie Grandmother or whatever Juliet would call her."

Juliet wasn't going to be around long enough to call Gwen anything. "And she thinks that if I have a baby in my life for a few weeks, I'll immediately hunt down a woman, get married and start a family."

"As ridiculous as that sounds, that's our Aunt Gwen."

He laughed. "I'm sure that is Gwen's plan, but she is looking for Veronica. I've checked the airline manifests and she's made several trips over the past week."

"That's illegal." Ellen smiled with him. "I'm glad not everything has changed about you. Tell me what you've learned about the scum trying to sell our Diva to our clients."

"I've heard lots of rumors on the internet about competing software but no one has been able to forward a name or even a possibility. I've also checked into the background of everyone who's worked for us over the past six months."

"Even our permanent employees?" Ellen sounded shocked.

"Yes."

"What did you find?"

"Nothing. Nothing suspicious. Walter's taken out a big

loan for his new house, but between the salary he and his wife make it's not unreasonable."

Ellen opened her mouth, closed it and then opened it again. "I hate this. His wife is on maternity leave. And I know that she would like to stay home with their child and have several more. We had a long talk about it at her baby shower."

"So he does have financial reasons." Sam hated to think that someone they knew, they trusted, was betraying them.

"I don't like this. Being suspicious of people we've known for years. People who are our friends!"

"Someone is trying to steal Diva."

Ellen twirled a strand of hair around one finger as she assessed his words. "Have there been any other occurrences?"

"There was one. I didn't want to tell you about it over the phone, because I wasn't sure, but a few nights ago, last Friday, someone was in our offices again."

"How do you know?"

"I'm not one hundred percent sure, I was rather distracted by what was going on—" All the lovemaking with Anne was affecting his brain, but he wasn't about to tell his cousin that. "I set the security system and no alarms went off, but the next morning when I went to check on my computer, someone had been using it."

"How do you know?"

"I set a very simple trap. I put a pencil on my keyboard as if I had forgotten it there when I shut off the system. It wasn't on the keyboard in the morning. It was back on my desk."

"Are you sure?"

"Yes."

"But somebody from E² could have come back to work on their computer for a few hours over the evening and picked up your pencil."

"That's true, but I don't think that's what happened."

Ellen bit her lip as she processed the information. "Did the thief get the files on Diva?"

"If he managed to break into my encrypted files he would have gotten false information. I've moved all the real data on Diva onto this." He held up a computer disk.

"It's all on that one disk?" Ellen swallowed.

"Relax." He reached into Juliet's diaper bag and pulled out two more disks. "I believe in backup. This one is for you. And this one—" he put it back into the diaper bag "—we leave with the little innocent baby."

"I'm surprised you didn't put it into the diaper bin."

"I thought of it, but have you looked inside there? No, that's going beyond the call of duty. Besides, Anne keeps the diaper bag with her and Juliet most of the time, so our computer disk should be perfectly safe."

Ellen put her computer disk into her briefcase. "So you have one disk, I have the second and Anne has the third. Does she know?"

"No. I thought it would be safer that way. I was also thinking of hiring her brother on a temporary basis to help me with a few problems on Diva II."

"Her brother? Is that a good idea?"

"He arrived on the scene after all this began to happen so it seems like a good idea to me." Plus, he wanted to do it for Anne. He knew she worried about her brother. He'd made a few calls about Davis and learned that he was smart, but also had a very spotty work record. Usually when he quit he'd claimed he'd been bored, but the contact at IBM was a friend of Sam's so she had revealed a little more. She'd liked Davis's work, but there had also been something wrong. He'd disappear for hours during the middle of the day and there were a lot of phone calls from people trying to find him after he'd left the job. The men phoning for Davis had sounded…scary, she'd said.

Still, Sam would like to help him.

"I trust your instincts when it comes to hard workers," Ellen said. "Now when do I get to meet the amazing Anne Logan?"

"I'm here." Anne stood in the doorway dressed in butter-yellow leggings and a soft cream-colored sweater. "You must be Ellen Evans. I've been looking forward to meeting you." She held out her hand.

Ellen shook her hand firmly. "I've been looking forward to meeting you even more. Anyone who can drag my cousin away from the theoretical to the practical world has my complete admiration. Plus, I enjoyed speaking with you on the phone the other night."

"I enjoyed our conversation as well. I hope you didn't find my questions too personal, but it's important to get a complete makeup of any family you're entering into as the nanny."

"Yes, Sam says he would have been lost without you."

Anne looked at him and a soft, yearning expression crossed her face. Sam forgot to breath. "For a man with so little exposure around children, he did very well. I think he is quite capable without me," she said.

"Never," he said vehemently. "If Anne wasn't here I would have been at the nearest children agency by the end of the weekend."

"You two have survived over a week together."

"With Juliet." Anne corrected. "Now that you're here, perhaps you can convince Sam that he should go away this weekend."

"Away?"

"It's some kind of weekend with the boys. I gather they rent a cabin in Vermont, play a lot of cards, fish a little, drink beer and tell wildly outrageous stories of their great successes over the year. Especially with the women."

Ellen raised her brow. "You always go to the guys' getaway," she said to him and then explained to Anne. "A group of them began the tradition while they were in college. They all went to CalTech, but spread across the country after graduation. Now they meet once a year in the same cabin and do all that guy-bonding stuff. Tony Morris flies in from California every year just to be there. You only have a two-hour drive. What are you thinking of?"

He didn't have a good answer—he just didn't like to leave Anne alone, but he couldn't say that. Even Anne would wonder, as he had been trying to keep his distance from her over the past couple of days. She had noticed but hadn't said anything. Clearly she knew they were as wrong for each other as he did. "I don't like to leave Anne alone with the baby, and with everything that's happened with Diva…"

"Go," Ellen said firmly. "I'm here now to help with the baby. And we don't know when or if anything is going to happen again with Diva. Leave us women alone to get to know each other."

LEAVE THE WOMEN TOGETHER to get to know each other better, Sam thought as he chewed on the end of a cigar. What had he been thinking? By now Ellen had probably told Anne about every stupid thing he'd done as a kid.

"Are you going to bid or are you going to stare at your cards all night long?" Frank asked. "Pass the chips my way when you've decided."

"I'm out." Sam put down his cards and stood to stretch his legs. Frank raised the pot by five dollars and Tony matched him. Henry stared at his cards and didn't say anything but he matched the bid.

"What's bugging you?" Tony looked up from his cards to consider Sam. "You've been different all weekend long. Distracted-like. Is it a woman?"

"No. Sort of." Sam popped open the beer can and sat back on his chair. He wanted to tell his friends, but the story sounded so incredible. Plus, he didn't really know what to tell them about Anne. "I had this baby left on my doorstep."

"Hey, no kidding." Frank laughed. "Just like in the movies. Remember that one with the three guys, 'Magnum PI' and the guy from 'Cheers'."

"*Three Men and a Baby*. With Tom Selleck and Ted Danson," Tony corrected. As the producer of several syndicated game shows, he knew the entertainment business. In college he'd majored in business but spent all his free time at the movies or watching television. Entertainment trivia was as natural to him as breathing. Moreover, he didn't consider it trivia; he considered it vital information.

Frank chomped down on his cigar. "Yeah, Magnum and the bar guy. Plus the star from those *Police Academy* movies."

"Steve Guttenberg. And calling him a star might be stretching the point." Tony raised the bid again. He shook his finger at Sam. "A baby? Sammy, I thought you were more careful…"

"I am careful. The baby isn't mine. My aunt Gwen—"

"Say no more, Sam, we get the picture." His college friends had met Gwen and knew all about her meddling. Frank held up his hand and then frowned at his cards. "Damn, you'd better have a good hand, Tony. I'll raise you ten."

"Ha. You're falling straight into my trap. Here's ten and another ten." Tony tossed in a chip. His face was flushed with excitement and Sam was pleased to see his friend hadn't changed that much. Tony and Frank always played against each other as if their lives depended upon the outcome.

Henry looked up from his cards, stared at all three men and met the bid. His mouth moved, but he didn't say anything.

"Why did your aunt leave a baby on your doorstop?" Tony asked.

"Damned if I know. But the baby had a web page. That was how I knew she was meant for me."

Henry laughed and mumbled something.

"What did you say?" Tony demanded.

"Only that it would make a good title for a movie."

"What would?"

"Baby.com. A baby with a web page left on a doorstep."

Tony's mouth gaped, but then he grabbed a small notebook out of his pocket and scrawled into it. "Go on with your story," he directed Sam as he took notes.

Although feeling a little concern his life might become the script for a movie of the week, Sam continued. "The next thing I knew this nanny showed up and my life hasn't been the same since." Sam wondered what Anne and Juliet were doing now and then wondered why he was wondering. He was having fun with friends he only saw once a year, he wasn't supposed to be mooning over Anne and Juliet.

"A nanny? You have a nanny?" Frank's voice cracked with excitement as he put down his cards and waved off the bid. "I'm out. Is she any good, this nanny?"

"You can't be out," Tony protested. "You never give up."

"Anne? She's amazing. But my whole life seems to have turned upside down."

"She's good, this nanny? How long is she with you? Does she have another job lined up?" Sam thought Frank was going to grab him by the shirt and force the answers out of him. For an accountant, Frank could become very excited.

Tony called the hand and Henry showed his cards. He had a pair of aces while Tony had a straight flush and swept the pot toward him. Out of curiosity Tony turned over Frank's cards and saw that he had four kings.

"Hey man, you had four kings. What were you thinking?"

"Sam has a nanny. A good nanny. Damn, I left my cell phone at home—I didn't want to be interrupted. How stupid. Will you have her call me as soon as you get back to Portland? No, I have a better idea. I'll go back with you."

Tony stopped counting the poker chips. "A good nanny? Man, I know three couples who would kill for her name."

Frank glared at him. "No way. I knew about her first. I get first dibs."

Sam looked at Frank's pained expression and wondered what had happened to his friends. "Frank, you don't have any kids."

"That's okay. I've heard the horror stories. I was thinking we'll get the nanny first, get her used to our house and then we'll have the kids."

"You're nuts. Claire won't let you bring a beautiful woman into your house for over nine months."

"If the nanny is as good as you say, Claire will give up the master bedroom."

"The nanny is beautiful?" Tony asked.

"Yeah," Sam admitted reluctantly. "But Anne isn't the type to sit around for months on end doing nothing. First, she would redecorate your house, turn your living room into a counseling session for every local teenager and then organize arts and crafts sessions every afternoon. If you aren't careful she might decide to fine-tune your Porsche."

Frank leaned forward. "You don't know what it's like, Sam. It's a real cutthroat situation out there. I'll come home with you and make her on offer."

"Oh, no, you don't. I want her," Tony said in his soft, killer-producer voice, closing his notebook.

Sam realized that all of his friends had gone crazy. Well, maybe not Henry. He was looking at all three of them with a great deal of amusement. "What are you talking about, Tony? You're not even married. You don't need a nanny."

Slowly Tony blew out a smoke ring and grinned at

them. "This woman is beautiful and talented—I want to audition her. I've had this idea for a show and I've been looking for the right kind of woman to host it. Someone fresh and friendly who the average woman can relate to—not too yuppie. A woman that other women can also like. Someone not too hard on the eyes. A girl with spunk and ideas. Sort of like a sexy Mary Poppins." He pounded Sam on the shoulder. "Sounds like your nanny is my girl!"

"No, she's mine!" shouted Frank.

As Sam listened to the two men fighting over Anne, he realized he had no right to contradict them and claim her as his own. Not as long as he refused to let himself fall in love with the most special woman he'd ever known.

_____

10

_____

ANNE CAST OFF THE AFGHAN square and took a moment to
admire her handiwork. The varying shades of burgundy
would contrast Sam's stark decor very well and add a bit
of much-needed life into his beige living room. So far
she'd restrained herself from doing a lot to his apartment—she'd added a few plants and splashes of color
with some new cushions—but if she stayed much longer
she knew she'd be pulling out the paint chips and redoing
the entire house. A deep burgundy color on the walls
would look good in this room, accenting the black iron
frontispiece of the fireplace. Then she'd get rid of all this
bought-from-the-same-store beige furniture. If she could
only get her hands on this place and give it the love and attention it needed, it would look like a real home for Sam
and not just a place he slept in.

She counted stitches and told herself not to be a fool.

Lounging on a tan leather armchair, Davis quirked an
eyebrow as she cast on to her needle. "Knitting something
for the baby, I can understand. But an afghan for this
couch? I know you're a speed demon when it comes to
clicking the old needles, but even you won't be able to finish it before it's time for you to leave."

She bent her head forward counting stitches so that her
hair fell in front of her face, hiding her flush. "Of course
not, but I'll send it to Sam when it's done. Then he'll have
a memento of me and Juliet after we're gone."

"If he's like any regular all-American male, he'll remember you, Anne. Men don't forget you. Not only be-

cause you're gorgeous, but because after they taste your cooking…"

She threw a skein of wool at him. "If the way to a man's heart was through his stomach, supermodels would be out of business."

"Haven't you heard the day of the supermodel is over? It's true, I saw it on a magazine cover a few months ago." Davis patted his stomach. "Did you cook anything for dinner? Maybe your orange chicken or that stuffed pork tenderloin with apples and raisins?" he added hopefully, his blue eyes sparkling with mischief.

She shook her head. "You could eat most families out of house and home. I put a meat loaf sandwich into the fridge for you." She tied on the second color and picked up her cable needle. "You've practically lived here this weekend. It's nice of you to be so considerate, Davis, but it's also a little strange."

"Now you're hurting my feelings. If you didn't want me around, all you had to do was say so." He pulled a long face and stood up.

She held up her hand. "Don't be silly, Davis. Or course I like having you around. I'm just not used to it, that's all."

He sat back down and put his feet on the coffee table despite her glare. "With Sam out of town, I thought it would be nice for us to spend time together. After all, you'll only be here a couple of weeks more at most and then you'll take a job who knows where and we might not see each other again for months."

"It was nice. I'm glad you came over."

"You had a couple of more calls on my machine from couples desperate to have you become their nanny. One woman offered to fly you to Hawaii as a signing bonus. After some of the messages they've left, I wouldn't be surprised if Sam came home with one of his friends wanting to hire you." Davis laughed at his own joke. "I never realized nannies were in such hot demand. I may have picked the wrong field. Unfortunately when I was going to college everyone said computers were hot."

"Don't be ridiculous, Davis. You'd last exactly one day looking after three kids, getting them to school on time and making sure they cleaned their rooms."

"You love it, though, don't you."

"Yes."

Davis tapped his fingers against the arm of the couch, then looked up at her with concern on his face. "Just be careful around Sam Evans. I've seen the way you two look at each other. He's not the kind to fall in love."

Not the kind to fall in love. What did that mean? Did anyone ever plan to fall in love? Why wouldn't he fall in love with her? Just because she reminded him too much of Darlene? Damn, now she'd cast the wool too tight on her needles for the next square. At this rate, Davis was right—it would be years before she could send Sam his afghan. With impatient hands, she began to rip out the work she'd done and rewind the wool.

He would like it, though. He didn't have much that was homemade around his apartment. It was the small touches that made a place a home. And she wanted so much to make this place a home. Partly because it was what she did—the eternal meddler in her—but she was also doing it for Sam. He needed love in his life.

"Don't tell me you have a grievance against that ball of wool."

She dropped her needles and looked up to see Sam standing by the door. She grinned stupidly, feeling very happy to see his unshaven face and unkempt hair. "I trust the guys' weekend went well?" she asked, trying to keep to a minimum the breathy quality that always appeared in her voice when she talked to him.

"Yeah, it was great. Davis, good to see you again." Sam stepped in with his big strides and shook her brother's hand, making Davis look inconsequential beside him. "If you have some time this week, maybe you could come by and we could talk about some work we need done."

Davis smiled. "On Diva?"

"That might be a little premature. But we do have a lot on our plate at the moment and I'm always on the lookout for good talent. Your sister speaks very highly of you."

"She's a little too good to me sometimes. Listen—" Davis stood "—I'm going to the kitchen and pick up my meat loaf and then I'm out of here. I'm sure you two want to talk…about Juliet." He grinned wickedly, kissed Anne on the cheek and left.

She took a deep breath, kept her eyes off Sam no matter how good he looked to her starved gaze, corrected her knitting row and put down her needles. She met his gaze levelly, trying not to give away how happy she was that he was back. "I made some dinner if you want some."

"Meat loaf? With mashed potatoes?" He sounded as hopeful as a twelve-year-old.

"Yes. And glazed carrots. I put a plate for you in the fridge."

"Great. Is Juliet awake?"

"I'm expecting her to wake up any minute. You can go get her and bring her to me, if you like."

"I'll get her bottle as well."

With a smile he left, and Anne picked up her knitting needles again. What was she doing knitting an afghan for Sam? He would stuff it in a corner somewhere and never think of her.

She heard more footsteps on the stairs and then Ellen poked her head into the living room. "Oh good, you're here. I wanted to show you what I bought." She walked in carrying two large shopping bags and proceeded to dump the contents onto the couch. Material, with different patterns, stripes and flowers, but all in shades of green and rose, spilled over the couch. From the second bag she pulled out tassels and braids.

"Pillows. I'm going to design and sew my own pillows. You've inspired me with the project you organized for the neighborhood Christmas present-making club. Once I've got the hang of it, and have filled my apartment with original, homemade pillows, I'm going to make Christmas presents for everyone."

"What a wonderful idea. The materials are beautiful." Anne stroked a piece of velvet and then matched it against a piece of silk. "These two materials complement each other perfectly."

"I know," Ellen answered excitedly. "This is going to be so much fun. But I think I'm going to have to beg for your help. I'll be fine at the design, but fine stitchery has never been my strong point."

"I'd be happy to help. I think you'll be able to teach me a thing or two about design. And I love the idea of homemade pillows for Christmas. You can personalize with color and words and needlepoint and stencils. Maybe we could cut out a couple of patterns tonight—"

"Tonight?" Sam asked from the doorway. He was carrying a meat loaf sandwich.

"You shouldn't eat so quickly." Anne couldn't help herself. "It's not good for your digestion."

He looked at her funny but then smiled and bit into his sandwich. "Davis took my dinner. I traded him for the sandwich. There is something about meat loaf sandwiches that I have always found very appealing." He took another bite and swallowed. "Davis also passed along some rumors he's heard about Bill Madison."

"Yes, I've been hearing about his money problems as well. But he's just a kid, I can't imagine him stealing from us." Ellen sighed and began to stuff her material back into her bags. "I still find this whole situation—someone trying to steal Diva—too incredible. I'm going to talk to Carmichael again tonight and see if I can learn anything more." She stood and kissed Sam on the cheek. "You look perfectly disreputable so you must have had a good time. Was Henry as quiet as ever?"

"You would have hardly known he was there."

"And Frank was still determined to win every game even if he had to cheat?"

"He's gotten better at cheating—we only caught him once. And Tony was still full of plans, including one for Anne."

"What do you mean?"

"I told him about you. About how you helped Walter with his daughter who was finicky about what she ate. The neighborhood watch. The homeopathic doctor you recommended to Cynthia. The way you keep decorating my house."

She blushed. "I wasn't sure if you noticed."

"I noticed. And I like it. Anyway, Tony wants to audition you."

"Audition? I don't know..."

"You should do it, Anne," Ellen encouraged. "Tony is a great guy. If he thinks he can turn you into a TV star, he probably can. Most of the people in his business are really loud and so is he, but Tony means what he says. He'll be fair."

"A TV star?"

"Yes, you know that game show where you have to connect one celebrity to another with only three people..."

"'Three Degrees of Separation'?"

"Yes. That's Tony's show. I love it. Sam stinks at it, because he doesn't know anything about popular entertainment."

Sam swallowed more of the sandwich. "I know lots of computer games."

"He wouldn't know a movie star if he met one on the street."

"I would, too. I'd recognize Adrienne Barbeau immediately."

"See what I mean. A B-movie star from the seventies. Sometimes I think he's in love with Diva."

Sam licked his fingers and looked around the room as if searching for a piece of chocolate cake. "Diva is just as annoying as all women. I'm thinking I made a mistake giving her a female voice. I thought it would be more soothing."

"Ha. You figured that men were used to female secretaries and women would bond with another woman." Ellen finished stuffing her materials back into her bags and stood. "I'm the marketer, Sam—you can't fool me. Now, I'm going to leave the two of you alone. I'm sure you have a lot to talk about." Ellen smiled at the two of them as if she knew something they didn't.

"Don't be silly, Ellen. There's no need for you to rush off."

"Stay," Sam ordered.

"No." She shook her head, still smiling. "I know when I'm not wanted. I'll talk to you tomorrow, Anne. I'll come by in the afternoon and you can help me with my sewing."

"I'd be happy to."

Ellen waved and left, going down a half flight of stairs until she reached the door that would take her to the top floor apartment.

"Juliet was sleeping so I didn't wake her," Sam said as he stretched out on his leather chair.

Anne felt as if she was going to explode with excitement when he didn't say anymore. Finally she couldn't take it. "A TV show. This sounds unreal."

"If Tony likes you, he can make it happen. He wants to stop by tomorrow morning to talk to you, and then if you both like each other, he's going to shoot an audition tape."

Anne had no idea whether or not she wanted to be on TV. It sounded exciting but scary. "I'm a nanny. Why would he want me?"

"It turns out everyone wants a good nanny, or so I learned this weekend. But I told Tony about you. He thought you could be a much friendlier, more accessible Martha Stewart-type, with the addition of all the childcare information you have. Like what you told Walter when his daughter didn't want to eat."

"How intriguing. You mean I could talk about fussy babies and community service."

"And meat loaf recipes. You can't forget the meat loaf."

Sam grinned at her and she grinned back. Her happiness stemmed partly from her excitement at meeting Tony the TV producer in the morning, but more from the realization that Sam had been thinking about her, talking about her over the weekend. He had missed her.

But would he miss her when *she* left…for good?

"WHAT SHOULD I WEAR?" Anne asked, walking into the kitchen holding up two outfits.

Sam continued to feed Juliet without looking up at Anne. Juliet spit the apricot mush out of her mouth, but Sam ducked and calmly wiped her mouth with her bib. "You always look good."

"But should I wear a skirt or pants? My hair up or down? Lipstick?"

"A skirt, one of the those flowered ones, your hair down. Pink lipstick."

She gaped at him as he still hadn't looked at her. "Are you always this decisive?"

"Usually." He gave Juliet the spoon so she could bang it on the table of the feeding chair, and looked up at Anne, his dark eyes flashing with amusement. "It's even easier when the question is you. I like it when you wear those skirts. You look really soft and feminine and sexy."

"Why did I ever agree to this?"

"Because it's a challenge. You're very smart. You like to learn new things."

"Yes. Maybe. I don't know. All I know is you've really

confused me. Tell me again, exactly what you told him.
And what he said to you."

Sam lifted Juliet and rubbed her shoulder until she
burped. "I've told you five times everything we talked
about. Don't worry, he's going to love you. Here." He
started to pass Juliet to her but stopped when he saw she
was still holding two hangers of clothing. "Go get
changed. I'll go downstairs with Juliet and wait for Tony."
He left and Anne went back to her room and got dressed.
She studied herself in the mirror, dressed in a long pink
skirt that clung to her thighs and twirled around as she
walked, and a pink V-necked sweater. "Very pink," she
told her reflection and stuck out her tongue. "This will
have to do." She took a deep breath and went out to meet
Tony.

Tony turned out to be a delight. He was short and
stocky and unable to sit still. His foot twitched or he
played with his mustache. He surprised her by not taking
notes or even asking a lot of questions about her past jobs,
but instead just talked. And he was funny! He had lots of
stories about the celebrities who guested on his game
shows, but unlike so many people who liked to spread
gossip about famous people, Tony raved over the stars—
like the female sitcom character whose clothing hadn't arrived for a taping so she'd worn an audience member's
outfit and sent the audience member autographed pic-
tures from all of the friends in her cast. Anne found herself
warming to Tony, and after he excused himself briefly to
phone his grandmother, she told him about her Grannie
Wilton's famous peach preserves. "She won the blue ribbon at the state fair every year she entered, and I was the
only person she gave the recipe to."

Tony smacked his lips. "I don't think I've had homemade peach preserves in years."

"I'll make you some next year. Leave me your card and
I'll send some to you."

"That's a deal. But maybe you could demonstrate Grannie Wilton's technique on your TV show."

"I still can't believe you want me to be on a TV show."

"I've been thinking about it for a couple of years, and every time a new lifestyle show airs, I hold my breath. But no one—other than Martha Stewart, of course—has really hit the right combination. It all depends upon the host."

"And you think I might be the right host." She really couldn't believe that was what Tony believed.

"You're pretty and have a nice air about you, but I won't know the answer to your question until I see you on tape. Some people freeze under the lights, against all the frantic activity behind the cameras and the instructions being shouted into your earpiece. A few special people shine under the same circumstances. If I'm very lucky, you'll talk to the camera like we've been talking now."

"I see." Anne felt a curious excitement in the pit of her stomach.

"So you'll come by the studio this afternoon? The local talk show is on break for a couple of weeks. I think they're hiring new hosts before they fire the old ones," he added conspiratorially, always being connected to the local gossip, "so I've been able to rent their space for a week. Maybe longer if you're as great in front of the cameras as I think you're going to be." Tony might be a powerful producer but he didn't hide his eagerness from her and Anne felt reassured. "In fact, this would be a great place to film the show permanently if it all works out...but I'm getting ahead of myself. So what do you say about our little test?"

Anne swallowed. "Yes."

Tony stood and clasped both her hands. "I don't like to say too much too soon, but...I feel lucky. You feel lucky, Anne Logan."

"But what am I going to do? For the audition." She felt nerves zing through her entire body.

"Show me how to make your grannie's preserves, and

tell me your stories about her. All you have to do is be yourself. I won't have fully worked out the show for this afternoon, but you're inspiring me, Anne. I haven't been this excited in a year about a new project. I'll draft up a segment and then we'll shoot it and see how the camera likes you." He held her face between two hands and turned her head slightly. "Perfect. If the camera loves you like I think it's going to, then we'll have a show."

ANNE FINISHED TAPING the sixth episode of "Let Annie Help"—the name Tony had come up with for the show. He'd declared it was friendly and straightforward. She accepted a coffee from a production assistant and sank into one of the chairs on the set.

She could hardly believe Tony's little "test" show had snowballed into the six episodes that he would try to sell. As he smiled at her from off-camera, she could see him talking on his cell phone and punching numbers into his calculator. The man was a constant deal-maker. The makeup girl had told her that Tony had offered the morning show producer his services if the producer couldn't find suitable new hosts for the talk show. "I know everyone," Tony had told the bewildered producer.

"Perfect." Tony beamed at her, rocking back and forth on the balls of his feet. "It was absolutely perfect."

"It was fun." Anne slipped her feet out of the high heels she had worn, the only cosmetic change Tony had asked for, and rubbed her sore toes. The show had been good but exhausting. First, she'd had to control seven five-year-olds as she'd exhibited cooking that kids could do. That had been followed by a story and a demonstration of puppet making.

"It was more than fun. It was brilliant. It was warm and moving and sheer entertainment. The shots of the kids cooking were hilarious, especially when Timmy and

Sharon began throwing spoonfuls of pancake batter at each other."

"I don't think mothers who have to clean up the kitchen will be as excited."

"It made good TV." Tony kissed his fingers. "But when you used the puppets the little tykes had made to tell that story about friendship and the little boy who wasn't included, I swear I almost got a tear in my eyes. Made me think of phoning up my girlfriend and telling her it was time to set the date and start working on some kids."

"Do you mean you're getting married?" Despite the fact that they had been working closely together for over a week, Tony had never mentioned a fiancée. She knew he lived in Los Angeles, but traveled a lot, checking out local talent in what he called small TV markets, looking for an anchor or weatherperson who had the necessary charisma to step into a bigger market. "I didn't realize you were engaged."

"We're not. Not officially, that is." He checked off several items on the list on his clipboard—she had quickly learned Tony's clipboard was his lifeline. He frowned at the last item. "No, that's too complicated. We're not going to shoot any segments out of the studio, not until we've sold this show." He handed the list to the production assistant who was waiting for his notes. Anne waited for him to return to their conversation; she was becoming used to the way he worked.

"I mean I know she's waiting, but I've never asked her or anything," Tony said.

Just in case he was serious, because she'd learned he very rarely wasn't, she decided to tell him what she was thinking. "You can't call her up and ask her over the phone to marry you. She'd never forgive you."

"Why not? I told her I loved her for the first time over the phone."

"You did not."

"I'm always on the phone. She's a film editor. She knows what the business is like."

She raced to keep up with him as he walked over to a camera and checked out the equipment. Impatient, she waited for him to finish looking through the lens. "Are you sure she's waiting for you to ask her to marry you?"

"Well, yeah. Why not? We get along great and we're in love."

"But you don't make any time for her."

"I do, too. Whenever I have time and I'm in L.A., I...oh." Tony heard his own words.

Anne nodded in agreement. "Exactly. Your girlfriend, what's her name?"

"Linda. Linda Potter."

"She probably has a pretty full life back in L.A. She knows how to get along without you. How long have you been dating?"

"About two years."

"Hmm. Then you've reached a critical point. After two years, most women will assess where they are. Since you do most of your relationship over the phone, and probably cancel your dates fairly frequently—" she waited for his guilty nod "—then Linda is deciding whether or not she sees a future with you."

Tony rubbed one of his shoulders. "She was a little cool the last couple of times over the phone."

"Do you want to get married?"

"Someday, sure."

Anne cast a level eye on him and he met her scrutiny frankly. "I've always thought of myself as getting married. As soon as I was settled in my career and had some money in the bank. But there are a lot of deals I still have to negotiate and now your show—"

"Do you want to marry Linda? Could you see yourself growing old with her?"

"Grow old with her? Yeah, sure, Linda is great. She's

funny and smart and she understands my work, so most of the time she's not too bugged about it. Plus, she's got her own deadlines."

"Then if you want her, you need to propose. In person. With a ring. And you need to plan a romantic evening."

"Damn, I think you might be right. I can fly out in a day or two to do the in-person thing and plan a romantic evening, but a ring... What if she doesn't like it?"

Anne decided to take pity on him as Tony was now rubbing a knot out of his other shoulder. "If the ring comes from you she'll probably like it, but if you could describe her clothing to me and some of the jewelry she wears, I could help you pick out something."

"Would you? That would be great! Married. I kind of like the idea. Linda and me. And maybe some babies."

"If she says yes."

Tony paled. "What do you mean?"

"You're assuming she wants to marry you, but you've never talked about it. Maybe she's hung around for two years with you because she knows you're commitment phobic." Anne knew she was being a little cruel, but on behalf of women everywhere, she had to strike a little fear into Tony's overconfident heart.

"But she loves me, why wouldn't she want to marry me?"

Anne shrugged and took a sip of her coffee, stretching out Tony's misery. "You'll have to ask her to find out."

Tony rubbed a sweaty palm on his trousers. "Yes. I'm going to do that. And if she doesn't say yes, then I'll keep asking her until she does. She's the woman for me. We're meant for each other."

Anne patted his hand. "Let me know when you want to go ring shopping. Now, if we're done with the grand experiment, I have to get back to Sam and Juliet, of course."

Anne had taken a few steps away from Tony when he came out of his reverie and ran after her. "You know, picking the right engagement ring could be a good idea for a show." He wrote it down on his clipboard. "Wait, you didn't give me a chance to tell you… I sent your first tape to some of the bigger stations I deal with and they loved you. Honey, we're going to be in business together." Tony opened the briefcase next to him and passed her a sheaf of legal documents.

"What's this?"

"The contract I want you to sign for a very significant amount of money." Tony pointed to a figure that made her gulp. "Plus, I'll give you a percentage of the show. I like to keep the talent happy. You can take this with you and have your lawyer look it over—or Sam, he's pretty shrewd when it comes to business deals."

Anne stared at the numbers on the page. "I don't understand. Earlier today you said we were finished after these six shows. At least until you had a chance to put a deal together. I thought something like that took weeks, months." At least she had hoped it would, so she would have time to decide whether or not she wanted to become a television personality.

"Six!" Tony clasped her by the waist and twirled around. "This was just a test. I'm signing you up to a hundred episodes. I'm going to make you a star!"

11

"I DON'T KNOW, DAVIS. If I do the TV show then I can't work for a new family."

"It's a great opportunity—you can't pass it up." He got out of the kitchen chair, filled his coffee cup and helped himself to another cinnamon bun Anne had pulled out of the oven twenty minutes earlier. The tray was half-empty.

"If you keep eating those buns, you won't have any room for lunch."

"You sound just like Betty."

"Our nanny." She tilted her head thoughtfully. "Do you ever notice how we talk about her, our nanny, but not our mother?"

Davis shrugged. "That's the way it was in our family. At least our parents got us Betty. She was great. And they remembered us sometimes—although it was usually when they needed our picture to be included in the institute's brochure," he added with a dry chuckle. "Don't tell me that you're having problems with how our parents raised us, now."

"No, not really. But sometimes I do wonder... It's funny that Sam and I—the three of us, in fact—had very similar upbringings, yet we're so different."

"Genetics. And he didn't have a big sister like I did."

"He has Ellen."

"Yes. Is she single?"

She raised her head in surprise. "Yes, and she's wonderful but..."

"You don't think I'm her type."

"I don't really know what her type is. It's just that you usually date a woman for her more obvious physical attributes rather than for her personality."

"I'm getting older. Maybe I'm learning. I think maybe I'll ask her out for dinner."

Anne was pleased. As much as she loved her brother she worried that he never planned on growing up and taking on real responsibilities. If he became involved with Ellen, however… She pulled her mind out of her fantasies. What was she doing imagining them all together as a family? She would be gone soon.

She was merely pleased that Davis was learning to pick women of substance rather than women who were substantially endowed.

Davis swallowed another cinnamon bun. "I think you should do the television show and not just because of the money, although it is a lot. That is one heck of a contract. I wish I could have a boss like Tony Morris sometime. Think of what you could do with all that money. You could buy me a great car for Christmas."

She could buy a house, something old that held memories. Put down roots. She glued another acorn onto the centerpiece. Pinecones, fall leaves cut out of felt and twigs and branches completed the effect. Once she finished stenciling a pattern of leaves and acorns onto some inexpensive napkins she had picked up at a garage sale, her fall table would look wonderful. Moreover, the table would make a nice arts and crafts segment for her show. Darn, there she was thinking of the show like she was going to be doing it.

"Why don't you want to do the show?"

"It's never what I imagined myself doing."

"It's what you do every day." Davis considered his sister, and then reached out a hand to squeeze hers. "Anne, you're always helping people, making things like this, this—"

"Fall harvest centerpiece."

"Right. And you're always researching child care and health issues. That's what you've been doing on your show."

"I hadn't thought of it like that." She hadn't. She hadn't had much time to think since Tony had breezed into her life and begun to change it. It all felt a little out of control, but what Davis said was true. The show reflected her interests. And she could try to make sure it was entertaining.

She was afraid the show would change her. All her life she'd planned on taking care of other people's families until she had one of her own. Only she was almost thirty years old and didn't have a family of her own. Sam was treating her differently, putting distance between them. He hadn't touched her since he'd come back from the boys' weekend. He was already ending their relationship when it had barely begun.

She hadn't heard from Simon since their night out, but she suspected he'd sensed that her reserve during their date hadn't just been caused by a headache. Perfect husband material, according to her list, yet he'd been all wrong for her. Life sure had a way of not turning out as planned.

One of the acorns broke apart in her hand. "Maybe you're right, Davis. I'll think about it. I'm going to ask Sam what he thinks." When Davis smirked at her, she refused to say anything.

"Ask me what?" Sam stood at the doorway.

Davis grinned broadly. "She wants your advice on her new career."

Sam looked at her enquiringly. He looked so good, so strong and handsome that she wished he'd hold her tight against him. After all they hadn't seen each other for over eight hours. "Tony." She handed Sam the contract. "He wants to sign me to a deal for a hundred episodes."

"Are you going to do it?"

"I don't know. I liked doing the show, but it's different from working for a family."

"Where is he going to film the show?" She wondered whether he cared if she moved away.

"Tony said Portland was fine if that was where I wanted to live."

Sam remained silent as he turned to the second page of the legal paper. "It looks good. How soon would you begin working on the show?"

"In a couple of months. Tony said there was a fair bit of prep work to do. He wanted to sell the show to more stations and thinks I should meet with the creative team to develop ideas. A hundred episodes seems like an extraordinary number to me, but Tony said he needed a package to sell to the home and lifestyle cable stations. After the response he got to the first shows, he thinks 'Let Annie Help' will be a hit." The entire conversation sounded so weird and yet kind of exciting.

"So you could stay and keep looking after Juliet for another couple of weeks."

She considered picking up her fall centerpiece and smashing it over Sam's thick head. Not a word about him being happy she was staying in Portland. It had become clear that she needed to accept the hard, cold reality that the only woman he loved was Juliet. "I thought Gwen had found the mother. Last night she said that she was going to get the papers signed today," Anne said. She didn't want to remember how unhappy she had felt at the idea of her stay with Sam and Juliet coming to an end.

"Aunt Gwen phoned me downstairs in the office. The girl was gone from the address in San Francisco that Aunt Gwen had traced her to. Gwen wanted to know if I could keep Juliet for longer."

Despite the fact that he hadn't said a word about wanting her to stay, Anne Logan was a woman who fulfilled her obligations. "Of course I'll stay. I'll stay as long as you need me."

I'LL STAY AS LONG AS YOU need me. What had he gotten himself into? Or rather, what had his aunt Gwen gotten him into that he was now going along with like a willing accomplice. Gwen had offered to return to Portland and take over the care of Juliet but he had insisted she stay on the trail of Juliet's mother. Once the girl signed the papers he would make sure Gwen found Juliet a good home. No way in hell was he letting an overworked and inefficient bureaucracy take control of her life. He was going to be responsible for her. Afterward, when she had left him and gone to her new home, he'd check up on her every once in a while, send her a Christmas gift.

But what was he going to do about Anne? She'd agreed to Tony's deal and spent several hours every afternoon in the offices Tony had rented down by the harbor working with her producer and story editor. She either took Juliet with her or left her with Sam. He preferred the afternoons she left Juliet in his care—or rather in the care of everyone who worked at E². Juliet was an amazing child; happy and content to watch what was going on. But as Walter had told him, and which he secretly thrilled to, Juliet was happiest when she played with Sam as he worked. She would coo to the sound of his voice as he read aloud the equations. Sometimes she waved her fist when a calculation excited her.

He loved her.

Juliet, he meant.

Anne? That was an equation he hadn't worked out yet. After their two very explosive evenings together, he had kept himself away from her bed. As much as he longed to kiss her, to hold her in his arms as she slept, he didn't dare. An addiction should be broken as quickly as it could be.

Hell, he'd taken her to bed but he hadn't even taken her

on a date. Every time they were out in pubic together, as they were now, they had Juliet with them. Coward, his conscience told him. He was afraid if he pursued her, if he spent more time with her, he wouldn't be able to get her out of his head. She'd be stuck like an infinite loop in a program that never ended.

What would be so wrong with having an affair with her? If she was going to do the show, she'd be staying in Portland. She was about to have a successful career. Wasn't that what he wanted in a woman?

What he really wanted was Anne—in any form, manner or career. Her laugh. Her generosity of spirit. Her willingness to try new things. Her intense interest in the people around her.

All those peculiar craft projects he kept finding throughout his house. This morning he'd had to eat his cereal over the sink as the kitchen had been covered with more foam shapes and pipe cleaners than he'd ever thought there were in all of Maine. Then he'd had to look for space in the dishwasher between the baby bottles and baby plates. Before, nothing had ever cluttered his house. He liked the clutter that Anne and Juliet made. He wanted to keep that clutter.

He tripped over a nonexistent crack in the sidewalk and Anne stopped pushing the stroller and looked back over her shoulder at him. The sun caught the gold in her fair hair, pinned haphazardly at the top of her head, her clear blue eyes looking at him with such clarity he thought she would be able to read what he was trying to keep hidden in his own heart. "Is something wrong?" she asked all too aptly. "Are you worried about what's going to happen to Juliet?"

"Yes." It was partly the truth.

"Surely Gwen will find the mother soon. And she has a new family lined up. Has she told you much about them?"

"Just that they already have a little boy who's three and they want a little sister for him."

"A brother, Juliet, how do you like that? You'll like having an older brother." Anne lifted Juliet out of the stroller and the little girl's gaze connected with Sam's. He felt she was telling him that she wanted to stay exactly where she was—with him and Anne.

"Anne—"

"Anne Logan? You're Anne Logan, aren't you?" A small red-haired woman with a matching child on either hand stopped next to Anne. "You have that TV show. I saw you."

Anne smiled at her. "Yes, that was me. I'm surprised you recognized me—we've only taped a few shows."

"It was excellent. I made those wrap sandwiches and froze them like you suggested and now my husband takes lunch to work at least three times a week. He takes me out for dinner with the money he saves. Thank you."

"That's so nice of you to say. May I offer the suggestion of saving lunch money and taking you out to dinner on another episode?"

"Yes. That would be great." One of the little girls pulled on her mother's arm, pointing at Sam. "Shh, dear," the woman said quietly to the child, but Anne could hear her. "The man is big." The little girl stared at Sam and then smiled brightly showing her missing front tooth.

Thank heavens some women in this town had taste, Anne thought. "Your children are lovely," she said instead.

"They're twins and quite a handful, but I wouldn't have it any other way. This one—" the mother raised the hand of the girl on her right "—is Mary-Beth and this one—" she raised the hand of the opposite child "—is Louise. We call her Lulu."

"I love kids." Anne reached into the diaper bag and pulled out a small leather pouch. From it she extracted her business cards. "We're going to begin taping shows in a few months. If you call this number I could reserve seats for you and a friend for a taping. You could tell the studio audience the same story you told me."

"I will. I told my friends about you, but your show was only on the air for a week, so they didn't get to see it."

"It was a test run. But there will be more episodes, beginning in February, I think. I thought a Valentine's Day show to launch the series might be nice."

The woman let go of Lulu to put the card into her pocket and then pulled her escaping daughter back to her. "I'll be watching. And I'll tell my friends to watch, too. I have to lend the tape of how to make easy Halloween costumes to my best friend, Rosemary. She was traveling on business and her VCR failed her."

"I think I'll have to do a very special episode on the two hundred different ways to program VCRs."

The woman laughed. "Thanks. It was very nice meeting you and your husband." She took the hands of her two children and continued along the street in the opposite direction from them.

"How...nice," Anne finally said. "Several women smiled at me when I was shopping yesterday, but I wasn't sure if they had recognized me from the show."

"Looks like you're going to be a star." As he said the words he wondered how he felt about the idea. He'd thought Annie should do something more productive, more goal oriented with her life than be a nanny, but he'd been ignoring the fact that she was a great nanny. If he'd had someone like her growing up, he would have learned how to love.

Anne smiled weakly. "Yes. How peculiar."

"I ONLY WANT TO TAKE A FEW minutes of your time."

"You want to write an article about me?"

Sam overheard Anne speaking with another woman at

the front door. Her voice sounded taken aback and a little nervous, so he left his computer, picked up Juliet from the playpen next to his desk and went to see if Anne needed his help. The woman at the front door of the Victorian was dressed in a tailored black pantsuit that emphasized her slim figure. When she saw him arrive behind Anne's shoulder, she whipped out her hand and squeezed his, hard. "I'm Kendra Henderson, reporter for the *Portland Star*. You must be Sam Evans."

"Yes. I—" He moved his fingers experimentally, trying for blood circulation.

"I want to interview Anne Logan because we had a lot of queries at the paper about her." She turned her attention back to Anne and flashed her very white teeth. "Your show really impressed a lot of women. It's not every day a nanny gets her own show. I've done my research and learned that you've just signed a deal with Tony Morris for a syndicated show." She flashed her shiny big teeth at him. "Tony is a friend of yours. You get together once a year for a boys' weekend."

"Yes. I know Tony."

"Then maybe you'll agree to sit in on the interview and answer a few questions about how your nanny is about to become Portland's newest star." Kendra Henderson angled her body to the side, slipping past Anne, and started walking up the stairs to his apartment while Anne and Sam could only stare at each other.

He shrugged. "I'm sure Tony would be happy if there was a feature on you in the local paper."

"Do you think so? Maybe it would be good publicity. It's just that she's kind of..."

"Barracuda like?"

"Actually I was thinking more of the woman who sacrifices her own young to save herself. Then again, maybe I just didn't like the suit." She tucked her arm under his.

"Come on. If I'm going to spend any time alone with that woman, I want protection."

Kendra was waiting for them at the top of the stairs. "Shall we?" She tapped her toe as she waited for Anne to lead her to the living room. Since the reporter had chosen his tan leather chair for herself, Sam seated himself next to Anne on the sofa, tucking Juliet into his arms. She took one look at Kendra, scrunched up her face and decided to go to sleep. "What are you knitting?" Kendra's gaze had surveyed the room quickly and assessingly, stopping briefly on Anne's knitting basket.

"An afghan." For some reason, Anne flushed.

"The colors will look very nice in this room. You must be intending to live here for a while."

"I doubt that I'll finish the blanket before my assignment is done, but I'll send it to Sam once it's finished."

He sat up straighter at the news that the blanket was for his home.

Kendra took a notebook and tape recorder out of her attaché case. "Okay, I want to go over a few background details and then go on to discuss the television program." Kendra and Anne went over Anne's credentials, her education and the number of families she had worked for.

When Anne spoke about the different children she'd cared for, her voice softened. "Excellent." Kendra wrote some notes in her pad, then fixed her attention on Sam. "I'm afraid I'm a little confused about why you needed to hire a nanny. I checked your records and you're single with no children."

"I have the temporary care of a baby, Juliet." He indicated the sleeping child to Kendra, who flicked a glance at Juliet and continued writing in her pad. "Anne is helping me until the baby's mother comes back."

"How sweet. Now back to the TV show." Kendra asked a number of smart and thorough questions that Anne answered fully. Sam could see her begin to relax.

Kendra smiled at the two of them and flipped closed her notebook. "I think I have almost everything I need." She hesitated and looked down at her clasped hands, "But I have to admit that I'm wondering a little about the tensions between an attractive single man and a pretty single woman. I did a little checking and one of Sam's friends, a Bill Madison, said that you two are involved."

Anne stiffened her shoulders. "I don't know if involved is the right word..."

"We're not—" Sam stopped when he saw Anne's face.

Kendra turned her tape recorder back on and faced Anne. "You're sleeping with your boss. Do you consider that professional? Is that what most mother's should expect to happen when they hire a nanny like you?"

Anne jumped to her feet. "I'd like you to leave now. My private life is my private life. Besides, Sam is single. What we do, together, is no one else's business."

"Oh, I think it is my readers' business. They need to know the character of the woman they'll be watching and admiring on television."

Sam stood next to Anne and put his arm around her. "Anne Logan's character is beyond reproach."

Kendra Henderson smiled with feral pleasure. "Really. Perhaps you'll feel differently after you talk to Mrs. Paul Stone. She named her nanny, Anne Logan, as the other woman in her divorce petition."

Sam felt Anne stiffen as her breath caught. Whatever this reporter was talking about had to be a mistake.

Kendra reached inside her satchel and pulled out a piece of paper that she passed to Sam. He saw it was a divorce petition with Anne's highlighted name written in the paragraph of 'Cause for Divorce.'

Kendra smiled with satisfaction. "It seems to me we have a nanny whose expertise is more in breaking up marriages than helping families stay together. I'm sure our readers will be very interested to learn that Anne Logan, supernanny, is a fraud."

SAM THOUGHT ABOUT PICKING up Kendra by her collar and throwing her out of his house. She'd look good sprawled over his front lawn. "What are you talking about?" The steel in his voice matched the color of her suit.

Kendra tugged down a cuff and smiled up at him through her lashes, and he realized she was flirting with him. She was flirting with him and trying to sabotage Anne. He quashed the urge to throw her too-expensive attaché case after her.

"I'm talking about Paul Stone, Julia Stone's husband. The father of the last family that hired Anne Logan to look after their children. Only she became more interested in daddy than little Patrick. Julia Logan called Anne the Home-wrecker Nanny. It kind of has the sound of a good headline, doesn't it?"

Anne's face paled and she darted toward Kendra. Sam grabbed her by the shoulders and pulled her back to him, holding her against his chest. "How dare you make such outrageous accusations against Anne. Whatever crazy story you've picked up from who knows what source, you've made a mistake. Annie is one of the best people I've ever met and you're proving your own lack of worth by attacking her. From the moment I met you, I suspected a nice piece about someone doing good didn't suit your style."

"So the nanny's new boyfriend is a big tough guy." Kendra raised her chin. "I'm not going to get very far ahead writing silly puff pieces for the 'Lifestyle Section.'

But I've always prided myself on making the most of any situation. If you don't get the job you want, then turn the job you have into the job you want. For this story, all I had to do was some background research on Anne Logan, the woman all of Portland was growing to love. A real perfect little sweetheart. I didn't even have to break a sweat. All I did was check on your last job, back in Seattle. That divorce petition had your name on it."

Sam took hold of Anne's hand when she tried to pull away from him. He squeezed her fingers reassuringly and she looked at him in confusion, then smiled weakly. She turned back to Kendra, red burning in her cheeks. "The Stones were already separated by the time I arrived to look after their new baby and son, Patrick. Mrs. Stone hired me because she was going back to work and needed help as she was no longer living with her husband. I'll admit I was attracted to Paul Stone, but as soon as I realized there was a chance he and his wife might reconcile, I left."

"They reconciled?" Kendra hadn't known that fact.

"Yes. I hate to spoil your story, but Mrs. Stone canceled the divorce petition. She was angry when she realized that Paul was coming to visit their baby in the afternoon. Paul and I began a flirtation—she caught us together once and jumped to conclusions. I realize my behavior was unprofessional, but nothing happened between us."

Kendra pursed her lips. "Julia Stone stated that she caught you kissing."

"Yes, well, but it didn't mean anything." Sam heard the pain in Anne's voice and wondered what that meant. Had she fallen in love with Paul Stone? Had the man kissed her and broken her heart? He wished he could have a few minutes alone with the weasel so that he could set him straight. And learn what kind of man Anne would fall in love with.

Kendra tapped her pen against her notebook. "Let me make sure I understand this perfectly clearly. You and

Paul Stone weren't really involved. You were *sort* of interested in him, the two of you kissed at least once, Mrs. Stone was angry so she named you as the other woman on the divorce petition, but nothing was going on. And now you're *involved* once again with your employer. And I'm supposed to believe you." Kendra bared her teeth in a triumphant smile. "Your new relationship will make a nice addition to my story about you. The last thing I need is a good quote. Tell me, do you plan to sleep with all the men who employ you or is it something that just 'happens'?"

"You wouldn't—" Anne trembled.

Sam felt incredible rage, but he pushed that down, thinking about how best to protect Anne. He wasn't going to let this reporter hurt her. He held on to Anne's hand more tightly. "I'm afraid you don't have the complete story about us. I fell for Anne almost as soon as I met her."

Anne grew deadly still as Kendra wrote down Sam's words. "Sam, don't—"

"It didn't take me any time at all to realize I had a very special woman in my life—and that I didn't want to let her go."

"So the two of you *are* involved?" Kendra prodded, her pen poised over the paper, waiting to write down the words that could ruin Anne Logan's career.

"Yes." He took a deep breath, raised their tightly clasped hands to his lips and kissed Anne's fingers. "We're engaged."

"SAM SAID WE WERE ENGAGED."

Anne could hardly believe the words as she said them out loud. She'd waited until Kendra had left and then she'd checked on Juliet. Only then, after taking a deep breath, had she taken a puzzled look at herself in the mirror and seen a pretty woman with rosy cheeks and sparkling eyes. She should be looking aghast, horrified and bewildered by Sam's declaration, not like a woman in love about to spend the evening with her fiancé. Most especially not like a woman lucky enough to be marrying Sam.

She wanted Sam to love her.

He wasn't the commitment type. He preferred his work to people—his broken engagement to Darlene showed that. But over the couple of weeks that she'd known him, his actions revealed that he cared about Ellen and the people who worked for them. He cared for Juliet, as well, but not enough to want to keep her as part of his life.

She suspected that this whole mess was his aunt's plan: make Sam fall in love with the baby, learn to open his heart, be willing to commit himself to a woman. It looked like Gwen was getting her wish. But whatever emotions Sam was feeling were all mixed up. He didn't love her. He couldn't love her.

She wasn't the kind of woman he admired. He liked sophisticated, ambitious women, not women who talked too much and loved to bake. In fact, Kendra Henderson was exactly the kind of woman he wanted. Except he hadn't liked Kendra Henderson, not one megabyte, and especially not after she had begun her attack on Anne.

In order to rescue her from the woman's character assassination, Sam had announced their fake engagement. No matter what he really thought of her—or felt about her—he was a decent man and wouldn't leave her prey to a hungry reporter. He had told Kendra they were engaged to defend her. Face it, to protect her. Sam was big enough and strong enough to take her problems onto his shoulders, but she wasn't going to let him. Her mistake with Paul Stone was her mistake and there was no reason for Sam to have to suffer the embarrassment of a second broken engagement.

She took another look in the mirror and shook her head. Maybe she should put some rice powder on her cheeks to get rid of her rosy color. Unfortunately nothing would get rid of the shine in her eyes. "Don't be such a romantic idiot," she told her reflection. "He's being a nice guy, nothing else."

She left the safety of her bedroom, wishing she could just stay there and not talk with Sam about what was going on between them. Nor did she have any real idea how to broach the subject. Talking about feelings just wasn't in Sam's makeup.

At the living room doorway she stopped to look at him as he stood by the window looking out at the bay. "Watching the last of your freedom as a single man slip away?" She was pleased that her words came out firm even as she feared seeing his face, seeing the truth of her statement reflected back in his eyes.

He turned quickly to face her. "What do you mean?"

"Our engagement." When he didn't say anything, but kept his expression impassive, she became angry and decided to stick in the knife. Damn the man. He had to know what he was doing to her. "The baby."

He started and his gaze fell to her stomach. "Are you…?"

At the look of shock that crossed his face, she pressed her fingernails into her palm to stop herself from smiling. Truly she had never known she could take such satisfaction in torturing anyone, but Sam Evans was making her rethink her character. "I'm not pregnant. I meant Juliet."

"Juliet." He raked his hand through his hair. "I thought maybe…"

"It's only been a couple of weeks since we first… Plus I wouldn't even know yet if anything…" She stumbled over her words, pulled her mind away from the image of her and Sam making love…that only led to trouble. Or the picture of herself pregnant with Sam's child. "We used precautions…" Now that she had tied herself up into knots with this conversation, she wasn't sure how to get herself out of it. Still, she pulled herself together and smiled weakly at Sam. "I didn't mean to be ridiculous like this.

It's just that this whole circumstance has confused me. Perhaps, almost left me at a loss for words."

He laughed.

She pretended she hadn't heard him. "I appreciate you jumping to my defense with that awful reporter, but you told her we're engaged." Her throat suddenly became dry and she swallowed. "Betty always said lying leads to no good no matter how honorable the intentions. Even worse, she said that sometimes it becomes true." To his credit he kept his expression neutral, while she would have given anything to know what he was thinking. What he was feeling. "I could have taken care of myself, Sam."

"Were you in love with him?"

He surprised her with his question.

"Paul Stone. Did you love him?"

"No. I liked him, but I didn't mean to get involved with him. And we really didn't do much more except go out with their baby son, but Mrs. Stone didn't know he was coming over in the afternoons sometimes to see their daughter. I should have told her but it started off so casually, with him dropping by for an hour or two. And then I didn't tell her because I started to develop feelings for Paul. I thought he cared for me, but he really wanted custody of their children—and their nanny."

"What?"

She grimaced. "Paul was wooing me because he wanted to win the custody case and wanted to keep continuity of care. But Mrs. Stone caught us kissing and fired me. She was angry, not that I could blame her, and so she named me as the other woman on the divorce petition."

"You and Paul Stone weren't having an affair?"

"No. I had feelings for him and we kissed, but nothing else…I don't think anything more would have happened between us. It's against all of my rules, but I let my guard down briefly and Paul just kind of happened."

"That's why you didn't want to get involved with me."

She shrugged. "Out of the frying pan and into the fire."

"And now you're engaged to me." His dark eyes bore into her as he moved toward her, sucking all the oxygen out of the room.

"Temporarily." She brushed the hair off her face, using the moment to compose herself. "I could have handled Kendra by myself."

"But it was my fault she was interviewing you in the first place. Because I introduced you to Tony and he came up with the idea for the show, because of how much I talked about you."

"But I want to do the show." It was true. She hadn't realized how important the television program had become to her until Kendra Henderson had begun to say all those horrible things about her and she realized that Tony would have to fire her. As much as she loved being a nanny, the idea of doing something bigger was appealing. She could provide information to so many more people. The program meant she could learn about new projects, emphasize what she knew was important in child care, maybe influence politicians who made decisions about funding for day care and school lunches and all those other issues that always drove her crazy.

She would be more than just Anne Logan, nanny.

She stopped her crazy thoughts. She was happy with herself, with the choices she'd made, not unhappy. So where had this idea come from that she needed to be more?

The man who was causing her so many problems frowned at her as he continued. "Kendra would never have been checking into your background if you were still just a nanny. It's only because of all the buzz about your show that Kendra Henderson dug into your background."

What Sam was saying was true, Anne realized bleakly. No one was interested in her life when she was a nanny. Only when she was a potential TV star.

SAM GOT DRESSED FOR DINNER wondering what exactly he had said to Anne that had made her storm out of the living room. Fiddling with the tie, he half choked himself before he loosened the knot and restored oxygen. Finally he had the tie as it should be and put on his charcoal-gray jacket. He checked himself in the mirror, turned to go and then stopped. He looked different. He was still too big, and his face had the same firm chin and slightly crooked nose, but there was something...more appealing in the arrangement of his features. He looked...happy.

Standing stock-still, he met his expression in the mirror, one corner of his mouth quirked up as he shrugged. He was happy...because of Anne.

If, for once, he used the formidable intellect nature had given him for something other than his work, he would think of some way to keep her. Because Anne Logan, bless her loving, generous heart, was drawn to him; he knew that. She wouldn't have slept with him, or agreed to their charade of an engagement, if she wasn't.

Tonight, he'd make their engagement permanent.

He'd agreed to take over one of Ellen's business dinners with the ComputExtra people, so she could hang out with a group of computer hackers who met every few weeks for drinks in a local Portland bar. He'd offered to do the undercover work but Ellen had pointed out that she was much more attractive and *female* and would, therefore, have a much greater appeal to a group of dysfunctional nerds. In particular, she planned to get close to Bill Madison and learn what he knew, if anything. For some time, Sam had been thinking the culprit was someone other than Bill Madison. He hoped he was wrong. "If they've heard anything about Diva's competition, they'll enjoy telling me," she had said confidently.

She was right. Even better, Anne had agreed to accompany him to the dinner. Just like a real fiancée. Sam couldn't believe how well everything was turning out.

Since he and Anne were engaged—sort of—he planned to take advantage tonight and seduce her.

Making love to Anne had taken over most of his waking thoughts. He remembered what she tasted like, the sounds she would make when he touched her. After a stupid week apart, there was no way he was staying away from her any longer, and their engagement offered him a good excuse to keep his arm around her when they walked into the restaurant and squeeze her hand under the table as they waited for their food to arrive.

Sam found himself behaving like a love-struck school-boy as Martha Watson, the executive vice president of marketing for ComputExtra, smiled approvingly at him and Anne across the table. "You two are very good together. You remind me of Howard and myself when we first fell in love."

Anne speared an asparagus stalk with force and then darted her gaze to Sam and then back again to Martha. "Our romance happened very quickly."

For once Anne didn't have any more to say, but Sam was happy to jump in. "Anne is more conservative than I am when it comes to love. She believes in long courtships and working out the details of a relationship. Instead, I kind of swept her off her feet." Just like he was going to do once he got her back to their home

"And you?" Martha smiled benevolently at him, and he had never realized how easy these business dinners could be. All you had to do was talk.

"It was like magic. I knew right away as soon as I saw Anne that she was the woman for me. Just like when I get the answer to a complex mathematical problem. It was perfectly clear," he continued, starting to enjoy their story.

Anne attacked her potatoes and Sam was afraid they were going to go flying across the restaurant. Thankfully Martha Watson didn't notice. "Magic, that's nice. That's how it was for Howard and me."

Her husband took a sip of wine. "It was like magic after I'd been chasing you for ten months. She didn't notice me until I turned off the power in her office, leaving us stranded on the twenty-second floor."

"With nothing to eat or drink except a bottle of champagne Howard pretended he kept around in case there was ever anything to celebrate." She reached over and squeezed her husband's hand.

"I also had some candles."

"Yes. And it was magic. I fell in love with Howard that night. We've been together ever since."

Sam grinned back at Martha Watson and squeezed Anne's hand under the table again. While he was enjoying Martha and her husband's company, he wanted to be home so he could have Anne to himself. He wasn't satisfied with the quick squeeze of her hand he managed under the table—and that was only when he could wrestle her hand free from massacring her vegetables. He needed to kiss the arch of her neck and hear that little murmur she made before she climaxed. He wanted to make love to her until she began to think of their engagement as real.

He wanted to marry Anne Logan. Not that he really believed in marriage, or met the requirements Anne had drawn up for her husband, but he refused to lose her and he knew what it would take to keep her. She wasn't the kind of woman who would settle for an affair.

To keep Anne and Juliet, he'd agree to anything.

Anne must have realized that no one had spoken for several minutes. "Sam has told me a little bit about your company and its plans for Diva."

"Diva is the most amazing invention. It really makes a computer calendar useful for real people."

"Women like me who can carry it around in their purse," Anne said.

"Yes." Martha left all talk of love and romance behind as she launched into her sell job for ComputExtra. "I want to hook up Diva with digital phones eventually so you can have your phone and calendar in one small package, but until then, we plan to promote Diva I in a big way." Martha outlined their marketing plans including national advertising, hitting every age group from high school to seniors. By the time Martha had exhausted her plans they were on dessert and Sam was thinking he had to thank Ellen for handling business dinners like these.

Martha declined coffee and dessert and frowned slightly as her husband ordered a piece of triple chocolate cake, but didn't say anything. "I'm afraid I must have been boring you with my endless plans for Diva," she said to Anne.

"No, not at all. I find Sam's work very interesting."

"It's very important for modern couples to support each other's work. What do you do, my dear?"

"I'm a nanny."

Sam jumped in quickly. "Anne is too modest. She has her own TV show."

Anne glared at him but he couldn't figure out what he had done wrong. Instead he turned to Martha who was a very levelheaded, sensible woman—unlike the one who was living in his house. "Anne used to be a nanny, in fact, that's how we met, but she's just in the process of beginning to film a TV show. Kind of a self-help program with advice on parenting and crafts and things." He faded off as Anne's killer expression grew only more fierce.

"That's delightful. You must find that quite a change from being a nanny." Martha shivered. "Looking after other people's children, being at their beck and call. Why it's practically like being a servant."

"My families always treated me as part of the family." Anne pried her teeth apart enough for a false smile.

Martha blinked at her. "Why, of course, I just thought that since you were beginning a new career, you wanted the change. I certainly didn't mean to offend you. Our two children had a nanny—several, I'm sorry to say—but it isn't a profession I would encourage for my daughter. I'm sorry if I'm putting my expectations on you. I meant no offense."

"None taken. I love children. Looking after them has always given me a great deal of fulfillment."

"Yes, I suppose it could." Martha shrugged. "But then why are you doing the TV show?"

Luckily the check arrived and Sam signed for it quickly, wanting to put an end to this difficult conversation—and to get Anne home and into his bed.

She remained quiet in the car on the way home while he wondered if he should start kissing her the second they reached the porch or whether he should wait for them to be inside their apartment. After studying her tense shoulders, he decided to wait for them to get inside. He didn't want the whole street to see him get a slap on the face.

As she closed the door behind them, Anne threw her purse down on the steps and then stormed up the stairs. He followed her to the kitchen where she put the kettle on the stove and then remained standing by the kitchen counter, her back toward him. He went to her and brushed aside her beautiful blond hair from her nape, smelled that familiar and erotic vanilla and lavender and ran his lips along her neck. She stiffened and stepped to the side, away from him.

"What is it?"

She turned around and crossed her hands over her chest. She looked hurt. "You were very pleased when you told Martha about the TV job."

"I'm proud of you."

"But you're not proud of me when I'm your nanny."

He let out an exasperated breath. "I don't understand you wanting to look after other people's children, when there's so much more you could do."

"There is nothing that is more! I don't think you understand me at all."

"You're right, I don't understand. But it doesn't mean I think any less of you. Give me credit for having learned something while you're here."

"And what about when I'm gone?"

Now he had lost track of where the conversation was going. "You're not leaving for a while."

"It can't be that much longer. Gwen will be arriving soon for Juliet, then I'll be gone." She raised her chin and her eyes searched his face for...what?

"No." The word came out sounding harsh. "You don't have to leave. You could stay. You have the TV show—"

"Always that damn TV show." Anne ignored the kettle that had begun to whistle and paced the kitchen. "I don't care about the television show. I want to know what you want from me. Here we are, two adults, playing house. Pretending to be engaged." She brushed her hair from her face. "I don't know when my life got so complicated. What do you want?"

"I want you to stay."

"Why?"

"I care for you." She waited for him to say more. He took a step toward her and brushed the back of his hand along her cheek. She let him. "Besides, we're engaged."

"It's a pretend engagement," she said softly.

"It could be real."

13

"ENGAGED FOR REAL?" Anne could barely get the words out past her tight throat and then she waited agonizing seconds for him to answer.

He shrugged. "Why not? We get along. We like each other's company. We're great in bed together." He tugged gently at the lock of her hair he'd wrapped around his finger. "Do I come close to matching your idea of a good husband?"

The note of quiet worry in his voice gave her a small feeling of encouragement. "My husband is supposed to be in love with me." Her heart pounding loudly; she waited for his answer.

He let his hand drop and stepped away from her. "I don't believe in love."

At the monotone of his voice, the little bit of hope that had risen up in her fell flat, replaced by cool anger. He wasn't bitter about love because of Darlene, he simply didn't believe in it. She hugged her arms around herself to get warm. "How can you say that?"

"Easy. My parents were supposed to be in love and it ruined their lives. They didn't like having me much, either." He held up a hand when she opened her mouth to speak. "Don't tell me that every parent loves their child because it's not true. And the horrible stories you hear on the news every day about what a parent has done to their child only proves that fact over and over again."

He looked away from her, off into the distance, as if picturing himself together with the people who had brought him into the world. "I heard the story about my parents' romance often enough from my mother. It was her favorite bedtime story. They ran away together after they graduated high school and eloped because they were madly in love. My mother's parents disapproved of him because his family was poor. They disowned her and he joined the army right after they got married—just in time to be shipped overseas to Vietnam. Mom was pregnant when he left and she spent all her time waiting for him to come back home."

He stopped, took a deep breath and continued. "I think that's when the trouble really began, Mom being alone like that. She'd never been alone in her life. Plus, she had a difficult pregnancy, no one to support her, no real friends, certainly no family. She thought that love would get her through anything, but it didn't. I think she had some kind of a nervous breakdown when I was born, but no one talked about things like that at the time.

"What got her through their two years apart was thinking about him, imagining him as the perfect husband. But when Dad came back he was different. When he left he'd been a charming and optimistic man, but he came back disillusioned. It was probably post-traumatic stress. I figured this out years later, as did my mom, but at the time it was difficult. My mom couldn't figure out what happened to the young boy who left her behind."

Sam shook his head. "The man she married never came back. Dad was never that interested in me and Mom spent all her time trying to recapture those glorious first months of their marriage.

"Instead my father got into the import business and made a lot of money. A lot. And Mom learned to spend most of her time shopping, trying to buy something that would make my father love her like he had when they were kids.

"Finally Mom kind of lost it. She spent her time in and

out of resting centers. By then I was a child prodigy and everyone left me alone to think. Only no one asked me what I wanted. I wanted my parents, but they were too busy with Mom's problems and Dad's business to worry about me. Aunt Gwen was the only person who ever paid any attention to me as a boy, that's why I'd do anything for her now."

"Including looking after Juliet."

"Yes."

"How is your mother now?"

"I think she's given up on therapy, preferring month-long stays at spas and plastic surgery."

She wanted to wrap her arms around him and tell him how much she felt for the lost little boy he'd been, but she remained where she was. "I'm so sorry. But you can't compare your parents' relationship to everyone else."

"I studied enough psychology in school to know that we repeat our family's pattern."

Before Anne could bite her tongue, the words were out, "Is that what happened with Darlene?"

"My one ill-fated attempt at love. It was a disaster."

"You didn't love her? If you weren't really in love with her, then ending the engagement was the right thing to do. There's no reason to think you won't fall in love with the right woman."

"Someone like you." His smile twisted.

"The right woman," she emphasized. "Whoever she is."

"I thought the right woman was Darlene. I loved her. She didn't love me."

She felt like she'd been sucker punched in the gut. It seemed she hadn't been paying any attention to the facts whatsoever. "That can't be right. Everyone says you ended the engagement, plus you gave her the house out of guilt. At least, that's what I thought." She knew the color rose in her cheeks as she admitted she'd been snooping into his personal life. "I asked questions. I couldn't help myself. I was interested."

"I should have known you would have asked about me. I ended the engagement but not because of anything Darlene did. I just realized that she wasn't in love with me. She thought I'd make a good husband. I fit her criteria and she expected to fall in love with me." He shrugged. "She didn't."

"That's why you got so mad at me the first night. Because of my list. Like Darlene. I reminded you of Darlene."

"A little."

"But I still don't understand. What was Darlene thinking? Was she after you for your money?"

"Yes. No. I told Ellen she was only interested in my money but that wasn't true. The lie, however, salved my pride. But Darlene wasn't after me for my money, although I suppose it didn't hurt. It was simply a case of two people who thought they should have made a good match but didn't. I fell in love with her and she thought I might suit. When I learned the truth, I considered marrying her anyway. But then I remembered my mother and what a pathetic creature she turned into."

"Your parents married awfully young. And your father must have gone through a lot with his military experience. It sounds like they grew apart but refused to admit they'd be better off separate. Divorce exists for a reason. People do make mistakes."

"Logically I know that, but I wasn't about to make the same mistake with Darlene."

"You gave her the house."

"I didn't want it. We bought it together, planning our future in it. Well, she did most of the planning and the work on it. The last four months of our engagement all she did was show me color swatches and fabric samples while all I thought about was Diva."

"Darlene was recent?"

"Two years ago."

"You've been working on Diva that long?"

"Longer. She's been a pet project of mine for years. But it was only in the past few months that I got her to work properly."

"I'm sorry. About Darlene." Anne wasn't sure what else to say. All she knew was that she felt confused and alone and wished she could do something for him. For the first time, she was beginning to understand Samuel Evans. She reached out, stroking her fingertips over his cheek. He shot out his hand, wrapping his fingers around her wrist, holding her hand captive in his. He raised her fingers to his mouth and kissed them.

She was caught by the burning need in his eyes and by the flare of heat that raced down from her fingertips through her body. "I want you."

"Yes." She moved closer to him, letting the heat from his body envelope her. "I...I love you."

"No, you don't." His mouth covered hers fiercely. She dug her fingers in his hair and kissed him back with equal passion.

When they broke apart, she gasped, "Yes, I do. I love you, Sam Evans." She touched his hair, so dark and soft, and waited for Sam to say whatever he was going to say.

Instead he thrust her away from him, his expression bleak. "I don't want you to love me. I don't believe in it."

"It's not your choice. I do. I'm happy that I love you."

"You thought you were in love with Paul Stone."

"No, I never did. I was lonely and thought he was attractive but I was glad when his wife became jealous about me—he still loved her."

His lips firmed into a hard line. "You're not in love with me. You may want to be...to find yourself that perfect husband...and a father for Juliet, but that man is not me. I want to have sex with you. I don't want a happy family."

She felt his words like a blow, but before she could argue with him, tell him how wrong he was, how he might not love her, but she knew her own feelings, he was gone.

THE EQUATION wasn't working. Maybe if he changed the derivative he could... He stopped, throwing a pencil against the wall in frustration. *I love you.* All night long he had played Anne's words over and over again. *I love you.* The very idea that she really might love him thrilled and frightened him. Whatever emotion she felt for him, and he didn't doubt that she thought she loved him, Annie didn't lie to herself—it wouldn't last. If he let himself give in to her dream of the three of them together, happy, a family, he'd only be hurt worse when Annie realized what a mistake she had made. She'd realize it had been an infatuation with playing family—and then they'd both be hurt. And Juliet, she'd be hurt, too.

Juliet cried.

Odd how familiar that sound was now and how much he'd miss it after she was gone. Almost, almost he wished he could believe Annie would care enough for him to stay, but the last thing he wanted to see was her growing bitter, angry at him—and Juliet.

Sam picked up the monitor and listened to the noises Juliet was making. She wasn't upset or hungry, he could tell, she was just calling attention to herself. Letting the world know that she was awake and ready to play.

He left, racing up the stairs to his little girl. Funny how only a month ago he could never have imaged picking Juliet up from her crib and kissing the top of her head. "It's okay, little one, I'm here." He lifted her high in the air. She gurgled and then laughed with delight. Tucking her in one of his big arms, he began to explain the computer program he was trying to run, very unsuccessfully, and she listened intently. But as he explained the mathematics by rote, he looked around at the nursery, at the white clouds Annie had painted along one wall including a seascape mural and two little boats happily sailing the waves. The room was filled with Juliet's toys and sweet touches that Anne had provided.

He stepped out of the nursery and continued to walk through his home, studying the changes. It hadn't really looked like a home before Anne had entered his life, what, only three weeks ago. He could barely remember what those days were like, and he was not looking forward to them ending. And why did they have to end?

Why didn't he seize the opportunity that the fates had granted him? Was he really such a coward to let everything go?

He recalled every word he'd said to Anne last night and regretted them bitterly. In his work he was ready to take all kinds of risks and gambles to figure out the next step, and willing to accept a few setbacks.

Was he really turning into the old fuddy duddy Ellen had claimed he was becoming? A man willing to accept so little for his own personal life just so he wouldn't be disappointed when nothing better came along? He had a chance for something better. Why wasn't he willing to try?

Because he was an idiot.

Because he was in love with Anne Logan and he was afraid. She might be attracted to him at the moment, she might even claim she loved him, but did she really? She was an impulsive woman, generous in her feelings. What if she saw him as another one of her projects? Isn't that what he was afraid of? That once she'd healed him, she would be looking for the next project?

No, Anne wasn't like that. She knew what she wanted. If she claimed that she wanted him, then surely he should be willing to take the risk. What did love involve if not both security and risk?

Had he ever felt about Darlene like he did about Annie? Not really. He'd loved Darlene in a cautious, safe kind of way. She'd seemed like a woman who would work for him. One who wouldn't expect much of him. And she hadn't. And that was why she hadn't really loved him. And he hadn't been willing to fight for her, to make her change her mind, but had let her go. He'd regretted it briefly, but then returned to his life with a great deal of ease. Ellen had been more upset by his broken engagement than he had been and that was because she'd wanted him to be happy. Because she'd imagined a marriage would be good for him.

Perhaps marriage could be good—if it was to the right woman. If he married Anne Logan. Now all he had to do was convince her.

He was also going to stop trying to change her. No more pushing her into the arms of Simon, or talking about the TV show. Annie wasn't defined by her career; she was who she was. The woman he loved.

"GREAT, HONEY, JUST GREAT. That was the best show yet," Tony said as he wrapped Anne in a bear hug. "Have I told you that I love you?"

She ignored his words having learned the hyperbole of television. Extracting herself from his arms, she picked up her slim portfolio and opened it. "I have some ideas for future episodes. I'd like to get a marriage counselor on the show to discuss relationships."

When Tony frowned his entire face fell to his shoulders. "That's so negative. I hate when couples get on the air and complain about what he or she has done wrong. We want 'Let Annie Help' to remain fun. Informative but upbeat." He closed her portfolio and clasped her hand between his. "Honey, it's your personality that wins the viewers over. You don't intimidate or lecture your audience."

"You mean they like parts where I goof up." She smiled ruefully. "Like when my glue gun went ballistic and shot hot glue at the cameraman. I'm just glad he ducks fast." She squeezed his hand and then pulled her fingers free.

"No, Tony, I agree with you. We don't want a segment filled with arguing couples." She had quickly learned the important television rule of using the plural pronoun to get what you wanted. "We want a counselor who can offer advice on relationships, even if everything is working well—to ensure it stays that way. Preventive relationship care."

"Yeah, I get what you're saying. Preventive relationship care. That sounds good. Okay, I'll have the researchers give you a short list of three counselors and then you can meet with them and choose who you want."

"I get to choose?"

"Sure, it's your show and you have to be comfortable with any regular guest."

"My show." She said the words aloud as she went backstage to her dressing room, took off the stage makeup and joined her producer and story editors for the postmortem and preparation for the next week of shows. As much as she had liked being a nanny, she loved this. After finishing the taping of an episode she was as energized as if she had just made love with Sam.

Every show gave her a buzz. And ideas. They were pouring out of her. She could finally understand Sam's passion for his work. She really could offer good advice on her show in an entertaining manner. Not preaching to the audience but showing by example. And they were fun issues that generally involved traditional women's topics. Crusader Anne Logan. She never would have imagined.

ANNE WALKED INTO SAM'S home wondering what she would tell him. How to explain that he was right about her career—that she loved her television show even more than being a nanny—but wrong about them. Then again, he might be right. If he was going to fall in love with her, he should already be in love with her. There was no way to force his emotions. He might like being with her but that was it. Perhaps she should plan a show around it: So you thought you could make him fall in love with you… Now what? "Sam, I'm home."

He stuck his head out of the nursery. "I'm putting Juliet to sleep. We can talk then."

He sounded so serious and looked so quiet. Did he realize how he had changed over the past few weeks? How good he was with Juliet. How much more open his expression was, how much happier he looked. Hearing the phone ring, Anne went to the living room to answer it. "Hello?"

"Is that Anne?"

"Yes," she said, sitting down on the sofa, recognizing Gwen's voice and fearing what she had to say. Once she left Sam and Juliet, what chance did she have to win his heart? At that moment, she realized she wasn't ready to give up just yet.

Of course not, her heart argued back. When you've found the man who is the right one for you, you don't give up.

"It's Gwendolyn Parker," Gwen told her unnecessarily. "I have great news. It took me much longer than I expected but I found Ronnie this morning and we spent the day together talking about what she wanted to do."

Anne gripped the receiver tightly. "Is she coming back for her daughter?"

"No, I am. Ronnie has agreed to the adoption. I have a plane reservation for tomorrow afternoon, I'll be in Portland late afternoon. My plane arrives, let's see, yes, at 5:43 p.m. Can you ask Sam if he can pick me up?"

"I'm sure he'll be able to. If not, I can pick you up at the airport."

"Excellent. I'm glad that I'll finally be able to find a good home for Juliet. My lawyer has contacted her new family and Juliet's new parents are very excited."

She hated those words: Juliet's parents. "I'm sure they'll

be thrilled with her. She's a wonderful girl. I...I've fallen quite in love with her myself."

"Of course you have. I could tell from the beginning that you opened your heart to anyone in need. As soon as you walked into that hotel room where I was holding interviews I knew you were the girl I needed."

"My brother always said I cared too much. That someday I would open myself up for hurt. That I never protect myself." She had wrapped the telephone cord around her wrist and carefully she unwound it.

"Darling, is something wrong?"

"No, nothing's wrong. I've just been wondering what it is I really want."

"Don't we all want the same thing? To find some way to have a life that makes us happy and valuable to others?"

"Yes, that's exactly what I've always wanted."

"I know you'll find it, dear. You're a wonderful girl."

Gwen said her goodbyes and Anne hung up the phone. Damn. She didn't want Sam's aunt to interrupt the pretty little fantasy world they had created where she and Sam got to play house with Juliet.

She continued to stare blankly at the phone until Sam asked, "Who was on the phone?" He stood inside the living room, looking at her, trying to read her expression.

She wanted to throw herself into his arms, cradle herself against his solid chest, and have him tell her that everything was okay, that he would take care of her and Juliet. Instead she made her voice as calm as possible. "It was your aunt. She found Juliet's mother and is arriving tomorrow to take Juliet."

"Take Juliet?"

He didn't say he wasn't letting Juliet go. He stood there as solid and unmovable as ever and Anne realized she had lost. "Yes. Gwen will be here tomorrow to take Juliet to her new parents. What you've been waiting for." She stood and her legs held her. "Tomorrow my job will be done. I'll be leaving."

14

"YOU CAN'T LEAVE." Sam blocked Anne from exiting the living room.

She raised her chin to meet his searching gaze. "My job will be finished once Juliet is gone."

Sam's face was pale with a spot of color burning on his cheekbones. "You can't leave. I won't let you. I need you."

"Do you? Do you really need me? Or am I simply the first person that you've let down your guard with?"

"It's you, dammit." He took hold of her by the shoulders. "I need you."

"I'm not sure if that's enough."

"I love you."

She stepped out of his arms. He'd said the words, but she now knew how Sam must have felt when she'd said the same words to him last night. He wanted to keep Juliet and would do anything necessary to achieve that—she knew this in her soul. She had to wonder if he didn't care more for her as Juliet's mother than as his wife. If he didn't find it safer that way. "You don't love me. You told me so yourself last night."

"I lied. I was frightened of what I was feeling and what might happen between us. But I know I can't lose you."

"You're telling me you love me because Juliet is leaving."

"Yes. No. That's part of the reason. The idea of losing you and Juliet is showing me what I'm afraid of. I thought it would hurt too much if you fell out of love with me."

"I wouldn't do that. I would never betray you."

"I want to believe you…but there isn't much in my life to show that people who care will really stick around."

"Ellen has stayed with you. And so has your aunt Gwen."

"Yes, I'm beginning to realize I had more than I had ever realized." He took her hands. "If you're willing to try, I am."

"Oh." She didn't know what to say but she knew what she felt—a great and overwhelming happiness and hope that maybe, just maybe, they could have a future together. They could make such a happy family if he would only let them.

"Could I pass your list of requirements for a husband?" he asked lightly but his eyes were serious.

"I threw away my list after the first week of knowing you. Sam Evans, you are my ideal husband."

He swept her up in his arms and kissed her. She felt the world tilt and realized Sam was spinning them around. She clung to him, savoring his strength as she brushed kisses over his face, across his strong jaw to his earlobe. She bit his ear gently and then laved the spot with her tongue. He stopped turning but kept her in his arms.

"Annie, you're killing me."

"Not yet," she promised. "But I'm going to make you think you died and went to heaven."

Then they were in her bedroom and Sam was sliding her down his body and she felt every powerful inch of him. "My," she said softly to him, "someone is very happy to see me."

"I'm looking even more forward to seeing you naked."

"That can be arranged." Anne pulled off her sweater and then she stopped. Sam's hands were at the button of the back of her skirt but she clasped them between hers. "If you really want to convince me that you love me…"

He stopped and looked at her, his eyes dark with passion. "Whatever you want."

"I want control."

He didn't say anything, just looked at her curiously.

"You are always in charge." She loosened his tie and slid it off, wrapping it between her hands, testing its strength. "Tonight, I want the control. The first night we were together, you...my arms ended up caught in my dress...and I just gave myself over to you. You took over our lovemaking." She snapped his tie between her hands. "Tonight I want the control."

"You want to tie me up?"

"Yes."

He grinned, unbuttoned his shirt and took it off, revealing his chest, his strong shoulders and muscled arms. She licked her dry lips. He lay down on her bed, stretching his hands over his head, grinning wickedly at her. "Tie me up. I'm at your mercy."

With trembling fingers she used his silk tie to fasten him to the bedpost. She had never done anything like this before and was finding she liked it. Her fingers stumbled over the knot and he raised his head to nuzzle her neck, distracting her, but she managed to finish the binding. Pleased, she sat back, straddling him, smiling with satisfaction.

"Kiss me," he requested and she did. The intensity of the kiss left them both gasping for breath and he moved under her... She broke free. "I'm setting the pace," she reminded him as she unbuckled his belt.

"You're driving me crazy."

"Fair play."

She ran her hand across his chest, flicking lightly against each nipple, and felt him shiver under her ministrations. She was intoxicated by the smell of his musky skin, the texture of the fine hair on his chest. She was drunk on the freedom he was giving her. She was free to touch and explore at her leisure. She could take all night showing him exactly how much she loved him.

But even more importantly, she planned to show him how much she wanted him, needed him—with her hands, her lips and her body. She couldn't get enough of him. She ran her hands over his sculpted chest and then kissed the same path.

At his belt buckle, her fingers struggled with the metal, but then she had it undone and held his erection in her hand. She lifted her head, smiling down at him as she seductively ran her tongue across her bottom lip. "Is this all for me?"

Sam's face glistened with sweat as he met her challenging gaze. "Maybe I'm just too much for you," he teased.

"I'll do my best to…accommodate you." She stroked her hand across his hard length and saw the strain in his muscles as he involuntarily pulled against the silk binding him to the bed.

"Anne," he ground out.

"Yes?" she asked as she continued to stroke and tease him. "Can't you take a little…play? I seem to remember you taking your own sweet time when our positions were reversed." She cupped him and squeezed gently.

He gasped. "Kiss me," he ordered. "I want to feel your mouth against mine."

She did and he lifted his head so he could take possession of the kiss, his lips full and demanding. She answered his passion and realized his body was pressing against hers, his legs tangling with hers and she was falling backward. Sam had twisted them around so that he was on top and she was trapped by his body.

He grinned devilishly at her. "Now what are you going to do?"

She grabbed his shoulders to push him off but ended up holding him instead as she laughed. "Has anyone ever told you you have a problem with control?"

"There's one woman who's pointed it out a few times." He let himself be rolled again as she pushed him over so that she sprawled on top of him. She kissed him, long and hard, and his mouth mated with hers perfectly. When they finally broke apart, they were gasping for breath.

"I love you," he said.

A bead of sweat was trickling down one side of his forehead. The expression on his face was serious as he searched hers.

Unable to resist, she wiped moisture off his face. "Do you really?"

"Yes."

"Good, because I'm not intending to go anywhere—" She heard a loud banging on the front door. "Darn. Who could that be?"

"Ignore them. I think we have more important business at hand."

The pounding continued incessantly at the door to their apartment.

"I should go answer..."

"Kiss me instead," Sam asked.

She did but heard the door open. "Anne," shouted Davis from the bottom of the house as he raced up the steps.

"It's Davis." She climbed off Sam, picking up her sweater off the floor and pulling it over her head. "I'll go get rid of him."

She ran out of her bedroom, cursing her brother's incredibly bad timing. Sam tested the bonds of the silk holding him immobile but realized he wouldn't be going anywhere until Anne untied him. Not that he was complaining. He'd be willing to trust himself to Anne anytime. He'd told her he loved her and it felt good, as if he'd figured out how to miniaturize Diva II. But better, much, much better.

He was going to ask her to marry him, and then they would adopt Juliet. Anne and Juliet were worth the risk. While no one could ever promise what the future would hold, he knew he could trust Anne. She would never deliberately choose to hurt him.

Yes, everything was going to work out perfectly. His very own happy ending.

Anne stepped back into her bedroom, her eyes wide and frightened. She opened her mouth but no sound came out. "What is it?" he asked.

"I—" She swallowed and stared at him. "Davis is here."

Sam was about to say, of course Davis was here, when her brother stepped into her bedroom, holding Juliet and a gun. He pointed the gun at Sam as Sam pulled on his wrists trying to free himself. The bonds held tight. He managed to push himself so that he was sitting upright on the bed, his hands still tied behind him out of Davis's sight. The equation was starting to fall into place. "It's been you the whole time, hasn't it?"

"What do you mean?" Anne asked, her voice shaking as she continued to stare at her brother in shock.

"Davis is the one who broke into E^2 that first night and has been back several times since trying to copy my computer formula."

"No, that's not true. Davis wouldn't do something like that. Why it, it's industrial theft..." Anne's words trailed off as the truth of his statement began to sink in.

"I prefer to consider it settling some old debts," Davis told her. "I'm sorry, Anne, but it was the only way."

"You encouraged me to take this job."

"Yes, that was a fine piece of luck for me. You arrived to visit me just as I was getting desperate trying to figure out how I was going to pay back the money I owed. I made some rather unfortunate bets."

"All those phone calls you kept getting from those scary-sounding men."

"My bookie. Or rather some unsavory gentlemen who worked for him. When you got that call about working for Sam Evans I realized I could take advantage. All I needed was one program I could sell. Sam's rich—he wouldn't miss it."

Her eyes bright with unshed tears, Anne confronted her brother. "But you tried to steal Diva. It's like his child. How could you, Davis?"

"I'm your brother. Are you really going to let me get killed?"

"No, of course not, Davis, but you could have asked me for money."

"I don't think you have a hundred thousand dollars."

"A hundred thousand! That's more money than you make in a year."

He shrugged and Juliet let out a cry as she awoke to the tensions in the room. "I already lost a lot and then there was a particularly bad football bet."

"Give me Juliet." Anne held out her hands. "I don't want her close to you. She's just a baby."

"No, she and you are my safety ticket out of here."

"You wouldn't hurt Juliet. I don't believe it. You may be in trouble and caught up in a stupid situation but you wouldn't hurt her."

Davis scowled. "You don't know me as well as you think you do. I need Juliet for leverage. Your boy here—" he nodded at Sam "—won't let anything happen to Juliet. You can come with me to look after her, but I'm taking her and you. After Sam tells me how to access the information I want."

"Davis, you can't do this. Please."

Davis pointed the gun at Sam. "I could hurt your boyfriend. Although it looks like he's into that kind of thing."

Anne stepped in front of her brother, blocking Sam with her body. "There's no need for you to do anything crazy, Davis. The computer disk you want is in the diaper bag."

"Anne—"

She turned to Sam as Davis picked up the diaper bag,

upended its contents on the floor and leaned down to re-
trieve the computer disk. "I've got it."

Sam pulled against his bonds, unable to believe that
Anne was giving away Diva.

"I'm sorry, Sam. He's my brother—"

Davis grabbed her arm. "Come on, I need you to come
with me."

"Don't be ridiculous, Davis. Take the disk but leave me
and Juliet behind."

"No, you can stay behind if you want, but I need Juliet
for protection. Once I've delivered this disk to the people I
promised it to, I'll have the money I need to pay off my
debts and you can have Juliet back safe and sound."

"Davis, I can't believe you're doing this. I'm coming
with you. Give me Juliet." Anne righted the diaper bag,
threw its scattered contents back inside and slung it over
her shoulder. She looked distractedly around the room
and grabbed some of Juliet's clothing off the top of her
dresser. Then she moved to Sam and touched him on the
cheek with the back of one hand. "I'm so sorry, but he's
my brother." She kissed his cheek. He felt a tear land on
his skin.

"Anne, don't do this," he asked. *Choose me*, he demanded silently.

She stopped, then turned to face him. "Oh, my," she
said in a whisper, "I'm helping Davis steal your project. I
am so sorry."

Davis pulled her arm. "Come on, we don't have much
time. I'm meeting my buyers in less than an hour."

With one last look at Sam, Anne left with Davis.

15

SAM WATCHED ANNE LEAVE his life, with Juliet, and felt himself losing everything he knew was important. He couldn't let it happen. But she'd been forced to choose between him and her brother. He understood her choice; family was family after all. He was a man she found appealing, a man she'd said she loved, but when it came time to choose, she'd picked her own flesh and blood.

Diva was his family. He wasn't going to let a worthless piece of trash like Davis Logan steal it from him. He was going to stop him.

He pulled against his binds again, but the action was useless. Then he looked at what Anne had tucked next to him, behind his back. It was the handy pocketknife she always kept in the diaper bag—he had seen her pull it out of the bag often enough to fix whatever needed fixing. She must have put it there when she'd kissed him goodbye. In seconds he had the blade out and was cutting through the silk until he was free. He stood up, rubbing his arms to get the circulation back, considering his options. He could call the police and they would go after Davis, but he wanted to deal with him personally. Anne had helped him by slipping him her pocketknife, the least he could do was give her brother a chance.

Anne had known he would be free in minutes and coming after them. He recalled how she had stood in front of Davis's gun—protecting him?

Realizing he might have a chance after all, he picked up his cell phone, grabbed his shirt, raced down the stairs and out his front door to his car. Where would Davis have gone? Back to his apartment? It was the only place Sam could think to begin to see if there were any clues as to where Davis might have taken Anne and Juliet. If he were very lucky, Davis might have left the pair behind in his apartment while he concluded his business deal.

Once the buyers had the disk, there was nothing Sam could do. All the buyers would have to do was institute a few superficial changes to the program and there would be no way to prove it was Diva.

He flipped open his cell phone and called Ellen.

He quickly told her what had transpired and, after asking if Juliet was all right, she said, "But Davis wouldn't hurt his own sister or Juliet."

"No, I'm not afraid of that. But he is a desperate man. I don't want Juliet or Anne exposed to the people he's dealing with. They're the kind who will do anything for money. They would have no qualms about hurting either Anne or Juliet."

"But wouldn't Davis have thought of that?"

"I don't think so. He's so crazed by the trouble he's gotten himself into that he's not thinking straight. Under normal circumstances I don't believe he would ever put his sister in danger."

"Anne gave him the computer disk," Ellen said gently. "How did she know where it was?"

"Knowing Anne, she probably found it in the diaper bag the day after I put it there. I should have realized she would. Or maybe I did and wanted to test her."

"She never asked you about it?"

"No, but she undoubtedly suspected what it was."

"So she never gave it to Davis when she could have at any point over the past two weeks."

"No, but she didn't know he was after Diva."

"When did you suspect it was Davis?"

"I've been wondering for the past week or so—I realized he had access to the house and, therefore, our offices. Plus, when I spoke to my contact at IBM about Davis working for us, I began to realize he had money problems. He was, unfortunately, a good suspect." Sam knew that Ellen was telling him that Anne hadn't been her brother's accomplice. He'd known that all along. But when she'd been forced to make a choice, she'd picked Davis. He understood her decision—he really did. After all, Anne and Davis were family.

Just because he'd begun to imagine himself and Anne and Juliet as a family didn't mean that Anne shared his sentiments. However, none of that mattered at the moment. He needed to rescue Anne and Juliet.

Then he'd convince her to make him an important part of her life. This time he wasn't giving up without a fight because he finally had someone worth fighting for.

"What do you want to do now?" Ellen asked, echoing his thoughts.

"I want to keep them safe—whatever it takes."

"And Diva?"

"She's not my first priority. Anne and Juliet are."

Ellen let out a breath. "That's the smartest thing I've ever heard you say. Do you have a plan?"

He outlined what he intended to do, asking her to stay home to wait for him to call if he needed help. If he didn't phone within an hour she was to contact the police. Then he closed the phone and prayed it would work.

ANNE RAN HER HAND OVER the top of Juliet's head, more to reassure herself than the little girl as she stood in the middle of her brother's living room. She had lived in this apartment for a week with him, but now it felt like foreign territory. Her brother was a stranger to her. How could she have been so wrong about him? He had stolen Diva from Sam. Diva—Sam's brainchild, his genius in miniature form. She knew how much he valued his work—and she had helped her brother steal Diva. What must he be thinking of her now?

She shivered as she imagined how outraged Sam must be. But she hadn't known what else to do. She'd been so shocked. Davis. She knew her brother was irresponsible, but she'd never suspected he would stoop to stealing other people's ideas. She examined him with new eyes. "You're a coward," she bit out between clenched lips.

"I'm only doing what is necessary."

"How could you owe so much money?"

Davis had the decency to look chagrined. "What I lost just sort of grew out of control. Then it was too late to get out of it without doing something desperate."

"So you sent me to work for Sam planning all along that you were going to steal from him."

Davis shrugged. "I was hoping for the best. It wasn't exactly something I could tell my successful sister about. I never would have imagined that people would consider you the successful one of our family. Where's your family spirit in all this? You're the one who's always going on and on about family loyalty."

"When it's deserved," she snapped. "Now I know why you were so interested in asking Ellen out."

Davis cast his eyes to the floor.

She shook her head in disbelief. "By the way, who was with you the very first night when you broke in and knocked Sam unconscious?"

"Yes, that was really too bad. I had a friend with me who knew about the trouble I was in. He agreed to help me the one time. I left the front door open as I left that night so that Larry and I could get back in without disturbing the neighbors. Larry took care of the security program that guarded the doors of E^2—it's kind of his specialty. If only we had succeeded that night. Sam would never have figured out I had any connection to the theft, I would have sold Diva, gotten the money I needed to pay off the loan sharks and you could have finished your assignment without anyone knowing any better. You could have had your fling with Sam and that would have been that."

"But Sam surprised you the first evening and you knocked him unconscious."

"Yes, Larry did that. Sam walked in on us and Larry was forced to take action. I'm not sure if I could have. But that was it for Larry. He didn't want any more trouble. But then I saw the two of you getting involved and was able to take advantage of Sam's distraction to search again, but I couldn't access the Diva files. He'd encrypted them. I knew he would have a backup somewhere, but I couldn't figure out where. I searched the entire apartment the weekend Sam was away, but I never thought of looking in the diaper bag." He shook his head. "I should have realized the damn baby was the place to look."

Anne held Juliet more tightly to her. "Don't refer to Juliet like that. She's sweet and defenseless. I can't believe you would threaten her."

"I needed her as leverage. I knew Sam would be willing to give up his work for the two of you."

"Oh." Her brother's words shocked her. "How did you know?"

"All you had to do was look at him. He's crazy about both of you."

"I'm not sure—"

"Don't even wonder about it. He's in love with you."

Anne felt a glow from the top of her head clear down to her toes. "He said he was. I hoped he was…" Her voice trailed off as she realized whatever growing feelings Sam had felt for her would have been crushed by her betrayal. She had walked out on him—leaving him tied to her bed, no less!—with Davis and his computer program. She was very afraid she had ruined whatever chance they might have had for happiness.

She stormed over to her brother now and she punched

him in the arm just as she'd done when they were kids. "You've ruined everything."

"Calm down, sis." He backed away from her. "This can all still work out well for both of us. My buyer will be here in a few minutes." He held up the computer disk. "Once I have the money I need you can go back to Sam."

"I don't think he'll take me. Davis, you are such an idiot. I'm in love with him and you've made me an accomplice. I can't just show up at Sam's door and expect him to take me back."

Davis checked his watch. "My buyer will be here soon. You will stay and look after Juliet until we've concluded the deal."

Anne went to Davis's bedroom, wrapped Juliet more tightly in her blanket and placed her on his bed with pillows surrounding her so she couldn't roll over and fall off the bed. What was she going to do? Anne wondered. Davis wasn't going to get away with this, not if she had anything to say. But how could she stop him? And what about the money Davis owed? If she returned Diva to Sam, what would happen to her brother? Surely she couldn't let her brother be hurt?

She heard voices in the living room and walked to the doorway to listen. She heard Davis and a man she didn't recognize. The buyer for Diva. She wondered if Sam had been able to use her knife and free himself by now. Had he called the police and were they searching for Davis now? Since they were back at his apartment—Davis wasn't much of a master criminal returning to his own home—they wouldn't be too hard to find.

But what if Sam decided to protect her brother? Somehow she knew he would be willing to give her brother another chance for her sake. No matter what he thought of her now, Sam wouldn't call the police. Funny how she knew him so well.

But she wasn't going to let Davis ruin Sam's work. She

didn't know how she was going to rescue Davis, but her first priority had to be to save Diva. She walked out into the living room and glared at the dark-haired, overweight man who was sweating with happiness as he rubbed his palms together. She walked over to her brother and touched his arm. "Davis, you can't do this."

He stared at his feet. "I don't have a choice. I need the money."

"Come on, come on, let's get this over with. Who is she?" the man asked Davis.

"No one important," Davis said.

"Whatever." The other man shrugged and wiped his palms on his nylon pants. Certain men should be forbidden to wear athletic pants, Anne decided. He pointed to the gym bag that lay at his feet. "The money is in here. Now all I need is Diva."

"Davis, please don't do this."

"I..." Davis moved his head as if he was searching for an escape route.

She tugged on his arm gently. "We can think of something else. Don't steal from Sam."

He looked at her like the lost little boy he'd been when they were growing up and their parents had once again forgotten about them. She held her breath waiting. This was Davis's chance to be something better. He pushed back his shoulders.

"Come on." The man twitched. "I want the disk. Now."

"No," Davis said and Anne let out her breath. "I made a mistake. I can't go through with the sale."

"What?" the man asked, his voice rising. "You can't double-cross me now. I've got the deal set up and then I need to be on a plane in less than two hours. I'm not letting some sniveling coward interfere with my plans." The man reached into the pocket of his nylon warm-up jacket and pulled out a gun. Anne swallowed. She had seen enough guns in one day to last her a lifetime.

Davis stepped in front of her, protecting her from the man. "I thought I could help you, MacDougall, but I was wrong."

"Those men who want their money are prepared to hurt you pretty bad if you don't sell me Diva."

"I'm prepared to take that risk."

"Well, I'm not. I need that program and I'm willing to do whatever is necessary to get it—including using your sister and that baby as hostages. I know who they are—I did my research. Go get the baby," he said to Anne, "or else I'll shoot your brother."

Not again, Anne felt like saying, but she did as she was told. She'd seen Davis disappear into his bedroom with his gun and she went immediately to the shoe box, third from the left, and gingerly pulled out the gun. The third shoe box from the left was where Davis had always hidden his treasures as a child.

The gun felt heavy and scary in her hands. She wasn't exactly sure what to do with it, but she knew she didn't want to shoot anyone by accident. She opened the chamber and saw the gun held no bullets. She should have known. Davis would never have threatened them with a gun that was loaded. Feeling a little better about her brother, she loosely wrapped the weapon in Juliet's pink goose blanket and then picked up the baby, tucking the weapon by Juliet's feet.

Carefully, as if she were a new mother carrying her baby for the first time, she went back to the living room. Now Davis was looking pale and worried. "Don't do this," he told the man he'd called MacDougall.

"Give me the disk," MacDougall said, "and I'll leave these two at the airport. I'll give her a quarter and she can call you to tell you which terminal to pick her up at."

Davis had a disk in his hand. "I'll give you the program, but you leave Anne and the baby behind."

"Oh, no, you don't. The only way I'll know this is the real disk is if I take your sister and that baby with me."

"I'll go with you," Davis offered. "I'm the one who created this mess, I should be the one to finish it."

"You'll come with me?"

"Yes."

MacDougall considered Davis's offer. "If this program doesn't work like I promised," Davis said, "then I'll have the explaining to do. I'm more help to you than a woman and a baby. You've probably never heard the little one scream her lungs out."

"Okay, I'll take you to the meeting. Give me the disk." Davis handed him the disk as Anne bit her bottom lip worrying. She had to stop MacDougall but she was afraid. She stared at the disk that was the source of all her troubles. No, that was wrong. The program wasn't the problem; people's desires for it were. She blinked and took another look at the disk. It wasn't the one she had given Davis earlier; she had seen it often enough in the diaper bag to know. She raised her head and met Davis's gaze. His eyes flicked over to the diaper bag and she knew that he had hidden the real disk inside it. Even if it was too late, Davis was finally doing the right thing.

"Davis…" She didn't really know what to say to him. "Be careful."

"I'm sorry I got you involved in all of this." He kissed her on the cheek and whispered into her ear, "Get Sam."

"Come on, let's get moving. We've got people waiting for us." MacDougall motioned with the gun toward the door.

"You can put that away," Davis said disdainfully. "I've agreed to come with you. I'm not about to double-cross you. I need the money."

"Money. Never knew anything that motivated people more." MacDougall picked up the gym bag filled with money, unzipped it, stored the gun on top and closed the bag. "I'll be holding on to this until we conclude our negotiations." MacDougall opened the door.

"Stop," Anne said pointing the gun at MacDougall with surprisingly firm hands.

He laughed when he saw her. "Get real," was all he said as he dismissed her, and Anne realized she had lost her gamble. She held a gun she wouldn't shoot that held no bullets. Slowly she lowered her hands in defeat and took a look at her brother when MacDougall turned to the open door and ran face first into Sam's fist.

"Oh." Anne covered Juliet's eyes as MacDougall came flying back into the apartment and lay sprawled on the floor. He tried to get up but Davis tackled him and held him on the ground. Sam walked in, rubbing his hand, followed by Simon.

"Is that it?" Simon asked. "Don't I get to hit someone?"

"You could hit Davis," Sam suggested, "after we get the information we want from this guy. Let him up," he told Davis.

Davis rose to his feet and pulled MacDougall after him. The fat man was sweating profusely and when he saw that he was outnumbered, three brawny men to himself, he seemed to crumple. "You don't have anything on me," he mumbled.

"I think we have a lot on you. Copyright theft for starters."

"You don't have anything on me." MacDougall began to grow more bold. "You can't prove anything. I have half a mind to sue you for assault and battery."

"You scum." Davis grabbed the man by his neck and shook. "I'll testify against you."

Sam looked at him and nodded. "I thought so. Well—" he turned back to MacDougall "—Davis is willing to incriminate himself to put you behind bars."

The man licked his lips. "You wouldn't," he said to Davis.

Davis stood away from him, straightening his shoulders. "I would."

MacDougall turned back to Sam. "What do you want?"

"I want to know who you were going to sell to at ComputExtra."

The man thought about it for a moment and then said, "Martha Watson."

"Martha." The word escaped on a note of surprise from Anne. "But she had such plans for Diva."

"She knew that if she bought a supposedly competing program for a great deal less money than the deal Ellen Evans had negotiated, that she'd become the next president of ComputExtra. That's what she wanted."

Anne couldn't believe that Martha was the culprit, although she was becoming accustomed to the feeling of disbelief. "She insulted nannies, so I did wonder about her."

"Okay." Sam nodded at Davis. "Let this guy go."

MacDougall ran for the door, then stopped, turning around to look at the bag that held the money. "My bag," he said, looking at Davis.

Davis studied MacDougall's face, his own revealing regret. Then he picked it up and threw it at MacDougall, who caught it and ran out the door in one motion. Davis continued staring at the man after he was gone.

"That was the money you were going to make for selling Diva?" Sam asked.

"Yes."

"You could have kept it."

"No. No, I couldn't." Davis met Sam's eyes dead-on. "I was stupid before, but I see how wrong I've been. Go ahead and call the police. I'm prepared to tell them everything."

"He gave MacDougall the wrong disk," Anne interjected. "I know it's not much considering all the problems Davis has caused you, but he didn't hand over Diva."

"I realized how wrong I was a little too late, but thanks for your support, Anne." Davis hugged her and Anne blinked back tears.

"Are you going to press charges?" she asked Sam.

His face hardened as she looked at the two of them. "No," he said, "I'm not."

"But—"

"I'm not letting you off scot-free," Sam continued. "I want you to go to Seattle with me to meet with the ComputExtra board and tell them all about your deal with MacDougall and Martha Watson, then they can decide what they want to do about Ms. Watson."

"Sam, that's very generous." Anne wished he would look at her and say something about them, but he didn't.

"I think my job here is done," Simon interjected. "If you don't need me for anything else, I'm going to phone Ellen and tell her what's happened."

"Good idea," Sam agreed. "Ellen will be worried." He turned to Davis. "I'm going to take your sister home. We have to meet my aunt to discuss Juliet's future. When do you have to pay back the money you owe?"

Davis swallowed. "I have another forty-eight hours."

Sam nodded. "Call me tomorrow morning. Maybe I can help you out with the money."

"You'd lend me the money? After what I did to you?" Davis stopped and looked at Sam. He nodded at something he saw in Sam's face. "I understand. Thank you."

Anne didn't know what he was talking about. She was focusing on Sam taking her home so they could talk about Juliet's future. Wasn't he planning on giving her back to Gwen? "The computer disk is in the diaper bag."

Sam smiled. "Good." He picked it up and took Juliet into his arms. He touched Anne lightly on the back. "Let's get Juliet back home."

She nodded, not trusting her voice. She was even more afraid now than when MacDougall had been pointing the gun at her and Juliet. In a daze, she walked down the steps from Davis's apartment to Sam's car, buckled herself in as Sam put Juliet in the car seat, then he drove back to his house. During the drive he didn't say a word and she found she couldn't, either. She remained silent as they walked into Sam's home. Anne's nerves were so frazzled she had to retreat to the nursery and put Juliet into her crib. She smoothed down the errant blond curls and kissed Juliet on the top of her head. How she wished she could stay here forever and look after Juliet. And Sam. Finally she straightened and turned around to find Sam watching her from the doorway.

"I'm sorry," she said and he scowled.

"You didn't know your brother was the thief."

"No, but I feel responsible, especially since…"

"Since you left with him?"

"Oh, Sam, I didn't have any choice."

"Of course not, he's your family."

"But, I betrayed you and that was the last thing I wanted to do. With Davis being so desperate and Juliet and everything, I just didn't know what else to do…"

"I know," he said. "What do you want?"

"I want…"

He stepped in and took her hands. "What do you want?"

She bit her lip. "I want us to be a family."

The grip on her arms tightened. "Are you sure?"

"I've never been more sure of anything in my life. I felt so bad when I left with Davis. I thought you would think that I wouldn't choose you, but I just wanted to keep Juliet safe. I couldn't let anything happen to her."

"Of course not. I know that."

"You do?"

"I knew what your were doing. And I knew that even if I lost Diva it would be nothing compared to losing you. And Juliet. But most importantly you." Very gently, he brushed his lips across hers. "If you didn't feel the same way, I still wasn't going to let you go. I called Aunt Gwen earlier and told her not to come here expecting to pick up Juliet. I'm adopting her. If you don't agree to marry me, you'll have to stay to look after Juliet." She saw a twinkle in his eye. "Then I'm going to wear down your resistance with my sexual prowess until you agree to marry me."

"Yes," she said simply.

"Yes, you'll marry me?" he said very slowly and clearly, wanting to be sure of her answer.

"Yes, although I do expect a lot of sexual prowess to keep me from changing my mind."

"You don't have to do the television show," he continued. "You can work at something in the neighborhood if you prefer. I love you for who you are, not what your job is. I want you to be happy. Or we could have lots of children," he suggested.

"Hmm, lots of children is appealing but I think one after Juliet is a good place to start. And I do want to work on my television show. I love it. Plus, I have this rather neat idea for a home-based mail order craft business—using the crafts we exhibit on the show—and hiring stay-at-home parents." She laughed. "Who would have thought I could have it all—a career I love, a baby I love and a man I love?"

"Are you sure you want to spend the rest of your life with me?" he asked.

She ran her hands down the long, solid length of his chest. "You're going to be a perfect husband," she said and her husband-to-be bent to seal their future with a kiss.

_____ Epilogue _____

"BEAUTIFUL WEDDING, ISN'T IT?" Gwendolyn Parker asked her niece as they watched Sam and Anne Evans step out onto the floor to take their first dance together as a married couple.

"Beautiful," Ellen agreed. She turned Juliet in her arms so that the infant could watch her parents. Juliet gurgled happily. Ellen hated to admit it, but her aunt's meddling had worked out even better than Gwen could have hoped for. Since the day Anne had agreed to marry Sam, he had glowed. Her heart warmed to both of them. They deserved it. Juliet seemed to agree as she waved at the newlyweds. For once, Anne was so caught up in her husband's gaze that she didn't notice Juliet.

"Sam looks almost handsome tonight," Gwen said approvingly.

"Yes," Ellen agreed. Her cousin had stopped trying to hide his big frame and no longer glowered at people trying to make them stay away. "Anne told me that she thought he was handsome the very first time she met him."

"Imagine that," her aunt said with some surprise. "Now all I have to do is get you married."

Ellen's breath caught in her throat and then she exhaled slowly. "Don't get carried away here, Aunt Gwen. If I want to get married I'm perfectly capable of finding myself a husband."

"Not according to what Sam has told me."

"That traitor."

"Don't call him names, dear. He's only worried about

you. He told me you've said you wished you had a man in
your life."

She'd been caught by her own words, but she intended
to get herself out of this. "Ever since Sam fell in love with
Anne, he thinks everyone should be in love."

"Wouldn't you like to be in love?" Gwen asked gently.

Ellen found herself blinking back a tear as she watched
Sam twirl Anne. Other couples joined them on the dance
floor, including Tony Morris and his new bride. When
marriage-shy Tony had tied the knot with Linda, Ellen
had felt another brick in the wall of her singleness cement
itself firmly into place. She was beginning to think she'd
never chisel herself out. "Of course I'd like to fall in love,
but it's not something you can make happen."

"Maybe," her meddling aunt answered noncommit-
tally.

"Oh, no, you don't. You are not going to play with my
life like you did with Sam's."

"It turned out very well, though," Aunt Gwen pointed
out reasonably.

"Yes, it turned out very well. They are very much in
love and very happy together."

"And Juliet has two parents who love her."

"Yes, I admit you did good. But don't you dare..." Ellen
sighed. What was the use? Her aunt was going to do whatever she thought was for the best. She took a sip of her
champagne wondering if she should sell her half of the
business to Sam and move somewhere her aunt wouldn't
be able to find her. Could a person actually live in Antarc-
tica? Maybe a sheep station in Australia. Her aunt smiled
secretly at her, and Ellen couldn't take it anymore. "What
are you going to do? Have a man with a web page arrive
on my doorstep? Husband.com?"

"What a good idea," said Gwendolyn Parker as she
watched Sam and Anne kiss. She looked back to see Ellen
turn pale.

Husband.com. A very good idea indeed.

Looking For More Romance?

Visit Romance.net

Look us up on-line at: http://www.romance.net

Check in daily for these and other exciting features:

Hot off the press — View all current titles, and purchase them on-line.

What do the stars have in store for you?

Horoscope

Hot deals — Exclusive offers available only at Romance.net

Plus, don't miss our interactive quizzes, contests and bonus gifts.

PWEB

HARLEQUIN®
Makes any time special ™

WIN A DREAM

In celebration of Harlequin®'s golden anniversary

Enter to win a *dream!* You could win:

- A luxurious trip for two to *The Renaissance Cottonwoods Resort* in Scottsdale, Arizona, or

- A bouquet of flowers once a week for a year from **FTD**, or

- A $500 shopping spree, or

- A fabulous bath & body gift basket, including **K-tel**'s *Candlelight and Romance* 5-CD set.

Look for **WIN A DREAM** flash on specially marked Harlequin® titles by Penny Jordan, Dallas Schulze, Anne Stuart and Kristine Rolofson in October 1999*.

FTD

RENAISSANCE.
COTTONWOODS RESORT
SCOTTSDALE, ARIZONA

K-TEL

Temptation®

COMING NEXT MONTH

#749 THE LITTLEST STOWAWAY Gina Wilkins
Bachelors & Babies

Pilot Steve Lockhart thrived on challenges, and he was facing a big one. He'd just started up his own air charter service, when he'd gone and fallen in love with sexy Casey Jansen, the girl of his dreams—*and* the competition. He had to have her. And the newborn baby he discovered in his plane was going to help him....

#750 FOUR MEN & A LADY Alison Kent
15ᵗʰ Anniversary Celebration!

When gorgeous golden boy Ben Tannen offered Heidi-from-the-wrong-side-of-the-tracks Malone money for college tuition, she lashed out—with a bicycle chain! Now fifteen years later at their high school reunion, Ben wants an apology...and the chance to prove they'd make better lovers than fighters....

#751 ABOUT LAST NIGHT... Stephanie Bond
The Wrong Bed

When Janine Murphy sneaks into her fiancé's hotel room for a wedding night preview, she's in for a shock. The man she's sharing a bed with is strong, sexy, irresistible...but he's *not* her fiancé! Derek's the best man. And definitely the *better* man...for Janine.

#752 WANTON Lori Foster
Blaze

P.I. Alec Sharpe wanted to keep Celia Carter safe, while she wanted to be in on the investigation. Alec also wanted to make love to her, while Celia was determined to fight her wanton nature. The compromise? Alec would help her play P.I. if she would give in to their craving for each other...